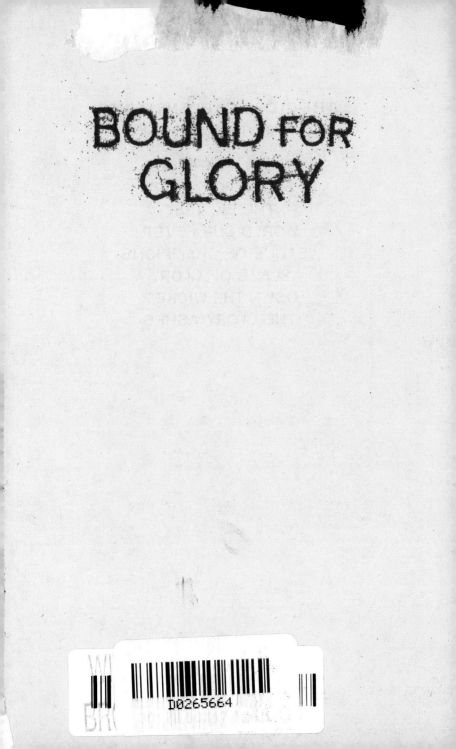

BOUND FOR
GLORY

THE GLORY GARDENS SERIES
(in suggested reading order)

BOUND FOR GLORY

BOB CATTELL

Illustrations by
David Kearney

RED FOX

A RED FOX BOOK 978 0 099 46121 0

First published in Great Britain by Julia MacRae and Red Fox,
imprints of Random House Children's Publishers UK

Julia MacRae edition published 1995
Red Fox edition published 1995
Reissued 2001, 2007

9 10

Set in Sabon

Red Fox Books are published by Random House Children's Publishers UK
61–63 Uxbridge Road, London W5 5SA,

www.randomhouse.co.uk

Addresses for companies within
The Random House Group Limited can be found at:
www.randomhouse.co.uk/offices.htm

The Random House Group Limited Reg. No. 954009

A CIP catalogue record for this book
is available from the British Library

www.**randomhousechildrens**.co.uk

Penguin Random House is committed to a sustainable future for
our business, our readers and our planet. This book is made from
Forest Stewardship Council® certified paper.

MIX
Paper from
responsible sources
FSC® C018179

Printed and bound in Great Britain by Clays Ltd, St Ives plc

Contents

Chapter One

"We're mostly a year younger than all the other teams," said Marty.

"What if we are?" said Frankie. "We're going to win the League – so smile!"

We were lining up for our team photograph before the big game against Barmewell. It was Glory Gardens C.C.'s first game in the North County League.

Back Row: Frankie, Clive, Cal, Marty, Erica and Tylan
Front Row: Jo, Matthew, Hooker, Azzie, Jacky and Ohbert.

My name is Harry Knight – you can call me 'Hooker' because everyone else does. I'm the captain and leading all-rounder of Glory Gardens Cricket Club – the best team in the universe.

What you see is almost our strongest line up. To be honest, we've only got twelve players to pick from. Jason Padgett normally plays for us but he's become really keen on chess and he's in a school chess tournament today – which is why Ohbert's playing. Marty calls Ohbert 'the worst number eleven in the world" and you can't argue with that.

Fortunately we've got some good players, too. Clive and Azzie are both brilliant batsmen and Erica, Cal and Matthew score plenty of runs. Erica's a useful bowler, too, but the opening bowling attack is usually Marty and Jacky with me as first change.

We're called 'Glory Gardens' because that's the name of the Rec at the back of Bason Street where we all started playing together. But we're 'officially' the Under Thirteen XI for Eastgate Priory C.C., the best cricket club in town. The Firsts have been County champions for the last two seasons. We're playing on the Priory ground today.

The big trouble with playing in the Under Thirteen League is that we're all really 'under twelves'. But there isn't an Under Twelve League this year in our area.

When the Barmewell team arrived, I could see why Marty was a bit gloomy about our chances. Mind you, Marty is always gloomy about everything.

"Cor, they're big!" said Jacky.

"Bigger than Cal even," said Marty. Cal's the tallest in the team. He's built like a fast bowler but he surprises everyone by bowling tricky, slow off-breaks.

"Look, it doesn't matter how big they are. We've got class on our side," said Frankie, our wicket-keeper.

"Yeah, a lot of great cricketers are small," said Azzie. "Look at Alan Border and Sunil Gavaskar."

"And Jack Russell and Brian Lara – not to mention Azzie

Nazar," said Frankie.

Azzie's our shortest player. He hardly comes up to Cal's elbow, but that doesn't bother him when he's got a bat in his hand. He moves his feet so quickly and I think his timing is even better than Clive's – though, of course, Clive wouldn't agree with that.

"We'll beat them, won't we, Ohbert?" said Frankie giving Ohbert a huge slap on the back which nearly knocked off his Walkman.

"Oh but . . . who?" said Ohbert who, as usual, hadn't been listening. You can see why we call him 'Ohbert'.

I gave Jo the batting order for the score-book and went off to meet the Barmewell captain.

Glory Gardens (in batting order) v Barmewell

Matthew Rose	Frankie Allen
Cal Sebastien	Marty Lear
Azzie Nazar	Tylan Vellacott
Clive da Costa	Jack Gunn
Hooker Knight	Ohbert Bennett
Erica Davies	

Close up Barmewell looked even bigger. Their captain was a red-faced boy called Dave Bickerton. We walked out to the middle and he spent ages looking at the pitch and poking it. We tossed and he won.

"You can bat first," he said.

"Thanks."

I don't know whether he thought there was something wrong with the wicket but I knew it was a good one. The Priory pitch is always good, especially after dry weather. I was quite pleased to be batting.

"Get your pads on," I said to Cal and Matthew. "They've put us in."

Kiddo Johnstone came over with old Gatting puffing and wheezing behind him. Gatting is an ancient mongrel and the model for the team mascot that my sister, Lizzie, made for us. He's almost round, short-sighted, rather smelly and black all over except for a sort of grey patch under his chin. Kiddo's had him for ever and they're always together.

Kiddo opens the batting for Priory Firsts and he's also the Glory Gardens C.C. coach. The bad news is that he is also one of our teachers.

Most of us – except Jacky, Matt and Clive – go to Hereward Middle School which is not far from Bason Street on the Hereward Road. Kiddo was our class teacher last year but he teaches us only French now.

"Remember it's twenty overs a side, kiddoes," said Kiddo. "Plenty of time to get a good look at the bowling."

Kiddo's great at training but his 'team talks' are not good news. He used to be a professional cricketer – a good one according to Azzie's dad – so he knows what he's talking about. It's just the way he says it.

"And don't forget what I've told you – don't try and knock the leather off the ball," said Kiddo. "The runs'll come quickly enough once you get your eye in." He gave a double thumbs up sign and walked off with Gatting waddling behind him.

"Remember, kiddoes," said Frankie, doing his not-very-good Kiddo impersonation. "Always hold your bat by the handle and get the flat bit pointing towards the bowler. And, if you like, you can give it a nice little pat after it has played a good shot."

"Oh, do shut up, Francis," said Jo. "I'm trying to concentrate on the scoring." She was writing down the weather conditions and the names of the umpires and all the other things which have to go in the score-book. Jo is the team secretary and scorer. She doesn't like to miss anything out. She gets very organised before a game with her pencils, rubber, pencil sharpener and her watch all propped up in front of her. Next to her sat 'Gatting', our so-called mascot.

I forgot to mention Jo is Frankie's sister – though you'd

never believe it. She's the only person I know who calls him Francis. Even his mum and dad call him Frankie.

Matthew and Cal were at the wicket. Matthew took guard and Old Sid Burns, the Priory's regular umpire, shouted, "Play."

The first ball flew past Matt's shoulder. It was quick and it spelt danger. We looked at each other. Frankie whistled.

"Outrageous," said Tylan.

The bowler took a ridiculously long run-up but his arm action was fast and high. The first over was a maiden. Six fast, straight balls. Matthew watched each one like a hawk. That's what you'd expect from Matthew. He doesn't have all the shots in the book – like Clive, for instance – but he doesn't give his wicket away easily. And he never backs off against fast bowling.

They brought a spinner on at the other end and Cal took a leg-bye from the first ball to open the Glory Gardens scoring. Matthew played the next five balls carefully. A second maiden.

"Another great Test Match innings from Matthew," sighed Frankie.

"You can't blame him for being careful against bowling like this," said Erica.

"There's such a thing as too careful," said Tylan.

That's obviously what Cal thought. The quick bowler – his name was down in the score-book as 'B. Silver' – sent down a short one just outside the off-stump and Cal cut it hard for four. The next ball was a fast yorker on middle stump but Cal got his bat down just in time and it flicked off an inside edge for four more.

Cal looked up and grinned, "Good ball." But Silver wasn't amused. He bowled a short, fast bouncer which rose head high to Cal.

"No ball!" shouted Sid, judging that the ball had risen over shoulder height which it had.

Both Cal and the bowler were now getting really steamed

11

up. Silver was sweating and grunting and bowling very fast. Cal swung wildly and missed a couple of times and then he tried to drive the last ball of the over back over the bowler's head. He got it too high on the bat and gave an easy return catch. Silver threw the ball up in the air with a cry of triumph.

The whole Barmewell team surrounded him and there was a lot of hugging and high fives and slaps on the back. It was a bit over the top. Kiddo didn't think much of it. I could see him shaking his head.

"Look at them, they've gone barmy," said Frankie – he should know.

"The Barmies of Barmewell," said Tylan.

Azzie joined Matthew who was still having trouble scoring off the spinner. He was bowling a tight off-stump line and turning the ball slightly to leg. With his field set close, it wasn't easy to push a single.

"Hit him over square-leg," shouted Frankie.

"What? Matthew?" sneered Clive. "He's never hit a ball in the air in his life."

Matthew took a lot of stick for being slow and boring but there've been plenty of times when he's held things together for us while wickets were tumbling at the other end. I knew he was really one of our most important players.

Off the last ball of the spinner's over, Matthew played a lovely sweep all along the ground, but it only went for a single. Frankie groaned, "That means he keeps the strike."

The third ball of Silver's next over lifted a bit more than usual and hit Matthew in the chest. For a moment it looked nasty but Matt didn't even blink; he just waved aside the fielders and faced up to the next delivery. It was edged for a single past slip and Azzie took guard for the first time. He got a bouncer which sailed over his head. It wouldn't have been a no ball to Cal but Sid had no hesitation in calling it. It was definitely over Azzie's shoulder. The last ball of the over was also short and Azzie stepped inside the line and hooked it savagely for four.

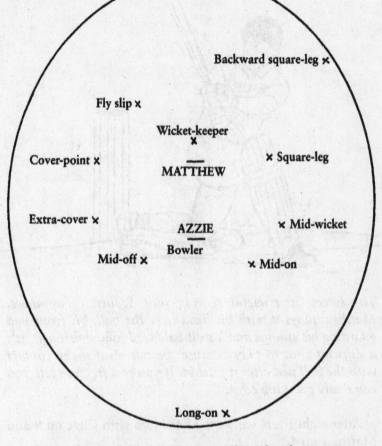

Backward square-leg ✗

Fly slip ✗

Wicket-keeper
✗
—
MATTHEW

Cover-point ✗

✗ Square-leg

Extra-cover ✗

AZZIE
—
Bowler

✗ Mid-wicket

Mid-off ✗

✗ Mid-on

Long-on ✗

This is the field that Barmewell set for the spinner.

He scored two more from a sweep played very fine against the spinner but when he tried the shot again he got a top edge and the ball ballooned into the hands of backward square-leg.

Clive came in, determined to get on top of the bowling right from the start. He drove Silver beautifully off the back foot for three twos in succession and then he was dropped in the slips attempting a cut.

The sweep is a useful scoring shot against off-spinners. Matthew plays it with his head over the ball, his front pad guarding his stumps and a well-balanced follow through. It's a difficult shot to play because the bat must make contact with the ball just after it pitches. If you're a fraction late you can easily get a top edge.

After eight overs we were 31 for two with Clive on 9 and Matthew on 4.

An over later we were 32 for four.

Dave Bickerton came on to bowl and trapped Matthew lbw on the back foot with a quick off-cutter. In came the captain and leading all-rounder. I played two classic forward defensive shots, but then I tried to force a shorter ball outside the off-stump and played it straight into my wicket. It was a stupid shot to attempt so early in the innings and I paid for it with a duck.

Instead of playing across the line with an angled bat (see dotted line), I should have moved into position and played straight with my body right behind the line.

"Give Clive the strike if you can," I said to Erica as she walked past me to the crease. "And don't play a stupid shot like that."

"As if I would," said Erica with a smile.

There was a lot of talking and nudging amongst the Barmewell fielders as Erica asked the umpire for 'middle and leg'. This often happens when we play teams for the first time.

"Erica's bringing out the silly side of the Barmies," said Frankie. They were laughing, whispering to each other and pointing.

"So, they think girls can't play cricket, do they," said Jo with a quiet smile.

It didn't take them long to realise Erica was as good as any of them.

Erica's played for us right from the start, so now we don't even think about it being strange having a girl in the side. There are lots of girls who are really good at softball cricket but for some reason they don't want to play in the league. Still, I was very glad Erica did.

The main thing about her batting is concentration. She seems to know instinctively when to attack and when to defend. She's got a good range of shots, too. Her cover drive played almost down on one knee was one of the best strokes of the game.

She and Clive batted well together for three overs. Then Dave Bickerton switched the bowling and brought on another spinner who immediately had Clive stumped attempting a big drive over the top. It's not the first time he's got out that way. Frankie was next and his first shot was an ungainly four over mid-wicket – that's how Frankie plays. Next ball he was out, bowled, playing the same horrible shot.

"Typical Francis Allen," sighed Jo.

Dave Bickerton came on at the other end and picked up the wicket of Marty – lbw for two. We'd limped to 55 for seven with six overs to go.

"If someone can just stay there with Erica we might still get 75 or 80," said Cal, half speaking to Tylan who was going out to bat.

Tylan did just that – for four overs he and Erica battled away, nudging singles and twos. But then both of them were out caught, trying to raise the run rate. That brought Jacky Gunn and Ohbert to the wicket with eight balls to go and 68 on the board.

"Not much chance of reaching 70 now – with Ohbert," said Marty, in a Martyish way.

Ohbert missed his first delivery by at least two feet. He was even further away next ball with an immaculate forward defensive stroke. This is Ohbert's favourite shot but the trouble is he shows no interest in the ball when he plays it. We call it the 'Oh-fensive stroke' – it's a sort of stabbing forward lunge with mouth open and eyes bulging.

Jacky hoicked a wild four off the last over and then took a single to give Ohbert the strike for the last two balls. He only needed one. The ball arrived and Ohbert swung with all his body, lifting his feet clean off the ground. This is his 'other shot' which I can't even try to describe. Somehow he managed to hit the ball straight up in the air. He stepped forward – looking frantically for a clue to where it had gone and then he found it as it landed – crack – on top of his baseball cap.

"Ouch!" cried Ohbert. The wicket-keeper made a despairing lunge to catch the rebound and Ohbert stepped back into his crease, rubbing his head and leaving Jacky furiously calling for a run and stranded in the middle of the pitch.

The keeper picked up the ball and lobbed it to the bowler for an easy run out.

"Oh but . . . it's not fair. I didn't know where the ball was," Ohbert protested.

Jacky shrugged and walked off.

"What a pair of jokers," said Clive as Jacky passed him.

"I'd like to see what you'd have done," snapped Jacky.

Clive just looked at him and smiled sarcastically.

INNINGS OF GLORY GARDENS   TOSS WON BY BARM.   WEATHER FINE.

BATSMAN	RUNS SCORED	HOW OUT	BOWLER	SCORE
1 M. ROSE	1.1.1.1	lbw	BICKERTON	4
2 C. SEBASTIEN	4.4	c & b	SILVER	8
3 A. NAZAR	4.2	ct ROWELL	SEAGER	6
4 C. DA COSTA	2.2.2.1.1.1.1.2.1.4	st MURRAY	BINLEY	17
5 H. KNIGHT		bowled	BICKERTON	0
6 E. DAVIES	1.1.2.1.1.2.1.1.1.1.2.1.1.1	ct McPHEE	BINLEY	17
7 F. ALLEN	4	bowled	BINLEY	4
8 M. LEAR	2	lbw	BICKERTON	2
9 T. VELLACOTT	1.1.1.1	ct SILVER	BINLEY	4
10 J. GUNN	1.4.1	RUN	OUT	6
11 P. BENNETT		NOT	OUT	0

FALL OF WICKETS

	1	2	3	4	5	6	7	8	9	10
SCORE	10	20	32	32	46	50	55	67	68	73
BAT NO	2	3	1	5	4	7	8	6	9	10

BYES	—	
LEG BYES	1.1	2
WIDES	1	1
NO BALLS	1.1.	2

TOTAL EXTRAS	5
TOTAL FOR	73
WKTS	10

SCORE AT A GLANCE

BOWLING ANALYSIS ⊙ NO BALL + WIDE

BOWLER	1	2	3	4	5	6	7	8	9	10	11	12	13	OVS	MDS	RUNS	WKT
1 B. SILVER	M	.44 9.M.4	1	222	✗									4	1	22	1
2 A. SEAGER	M	1	.1. 2W.	1.1	✗									4	1	7	1
3 D. BICKERTON	.W. ..W	..1 4..	✗	.21 2.W .1	✗									4	0	13	3
4 B. MAYER	2.1 ..	.+.2 ..	✗	1.1 1.	.4. 1.									3.5	0	16	0
5 B. BINLEY	1.W. 4.W.	.1. 1.1	.1 2.1	.W1 W..										4	0	13	4
6																	
7																	
8																	
9																	

Chapter Two

I had a word with Kiddo after our innings and he seemed fairly happy. "Keep the bowling tight and that could be a winning total," he said. "Mind you, I didn't think much of your shot, kiddo. A bit early to try and force one outside off-stump, don't you think?"

What could I say? I was just glad I'm an all-rounder. At least I'd get a chance to make up for my duck when I bowled.

Back in the Glory Gardens changing room, I found a huge row going on. Clive was standing in the middle of the room glaring at Jacky Gunn. "The trouble with this team," said Jacky, "is that there are too many prima donnas like you."

"I don't know what he's talking about," said Clive, looking round for support.

"Prima donna," said Frankie. "It's Spanish for a fat lady who sings opera."

"Italian," corrected Tylan.

"I know what it means," said Clive angrily.

"Then why . . . " began Frankie.

"Oh shut up," snapped Clive.

"What we need is a few more players who play for the team instead of for themselves," said Jacky.

"Like you, I suppose?"

"Like Matthew and Erica," said Jacky.

"If we all played like Matthew we wouldn't have scored twenty," said Frankie with a grin.

"Yeah!" said Clive, glad to get some support but surprised

to find it coming from Frankie. "Matthew clogs up the innings and then we have to take risks to push the scoring along."

"That's daft," said Jacky. "We'd got nearly fifty on the board off twelve overs when you threw your wicket away."

"Maybe you didn't notice I was top scorer," said Clive.

"Oh shut up both of you," said Cal. "We all know we should have scored at least 90. We'll just have to bowl better than we batted."

"Yeah, let's see big mouth *bowl* for the team." Clive scowled at Jacky and stormed out of the changing room.

"You shouldn't wind him up," said Azzie to Jacky. "You know what he's like."

"He gets on my nerves," said Jacky. "I'm getting fed up hearing how brilliant Clive is and how hopeless the rest of us are."

"That's just how it is with geniuses," said Frankie with a wink. He slapped Jacky on the back and smacked a cricket ball into his hand. "Come on, you can throw a few balls at me and pretend I'm Clive's head."

Clive can be a pain. He's always having a go at people without thinking how much he upsets them. But if anyone dares to criticise him he can't take it. Though, to be fair, he's been a bit better lately since he's lived with his aunt. I wondered if he was having trouble with his dad again.

I was more surprised at Jacky, though. You can't say he's ever got on with Clive. No one has. But he normally ignores him. That's his way – he doesn't say a lot; just gets on with playing the game.

Oh well, I thought. It'll probably blow over. And right now I had other things on my mind. 73 wasn't really enough on this wicket and we'd have to bowl and field really well to get a result. A lot depended on Jacky and Marty getting us off to a good start.

Their openers were the two biggest boys in the side, Ben Silver, the opening quick bowler and the captain, Dave Bickerton. They looked confident as they walked out to the middle.

Neither Marty nor Jacky is as quick as Ben Silver. Marty gets a lot of bounce and he can bowl a good away swinger. Jacky doesn't look much like a quicky; he's not very tall and he wears glasses. But he makes the ball skid through which surprises a lot of batsmen.

Marty bowled a good straight over; every ball was on the stumps, forcing the batsman to play at it.

Then Jacky came in from the practice nets end and his first ball was edged to Frankie who dropped an easy chance. The next was down the leg side and Frankie dived over it and it went for two byes.

Jacky walked up to Frankie and pointed to his gloves. "Do you know what they're for?" he snapped.

"Keeping my hands warm?" suggested Frankie. But Jacky was already storming back to his bowling mark. I walked over to him. After his argument with Clive he was really wound up.

"Get it on line first," I said. "You're bowling too fast."

I needn't have wasted my breath. The rest of the over was even wilder. It cost eight runs including two wides.

"Typical prima donna bowling," Clive said as I passed him. I don't think Jacky heard or I think he might have thumped him. Cal was having a word with Jacky – calming him down. It's good to have Cal around to keep an eye on things. He really understands the game. And the captain can't look after everything, can he?

I set a slightly more defensive field for Marty but I still kept the slip there for his out-swinger.

An outside edge went for four all along the ground between Azzie at slip and the keeper and then Jacky dropped a difficult chance in the covers. The ball was hit hard and low to his left and he got a hand to it but couldn't hang on as he hit the ground. He buried his face in his hands. It's strange how trouble follows you around sometimes.

At the end of three overs they were 16 for no wicket – it

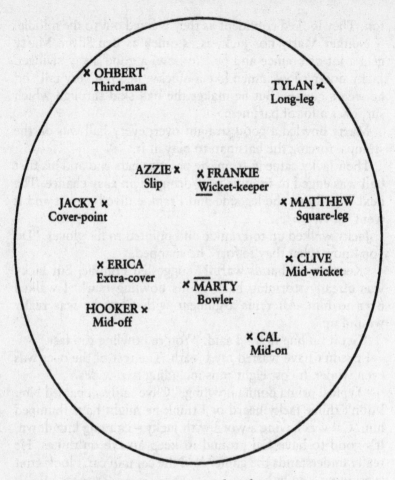

This is the field I set for Marty to bowl to.

would have been 16 for two if we'd held our catches.

Somehow Jacky pulled himself together for his next over but by now the two openers were seeing the ball well and our bowling didn't seem to be causing them too many problems. After six overs, I decided it was time for a change and I called Cal into the attack.

"I'm going to try spin at both ends," I said, "you and Tylan."

"You must be getting desperate," grinned Cal, taking off his jumper and marking out his seven step run up.

I looked at the scoreboard, 25 for none. Yes, I was beginning to get worried. We needed a wicket badly.

Cal got it. Ben Silver was completely fooled by the pace of his second ball. Cal pushed the first one through quickly but the next he bowled at his normal pace which is very slow with lots of loop. The batsman played all round it and it turned and hit middle stump.

"Outrageous bowling change," said Tylan.

It would have been an even better one if Marty hadn't dropped a straightforward catch at square-leg off the last ball of the over. That was three catches we'd put down.

Tylan opened with a wide and then another loose one, short down the leg side which the batsman swung away for four. There's always a risk that a leg spinner'll give away a lot of runs but, with Tylan, it's often worth the risk. His fifth ball pitched on a length, turned and beat the bat. It just clipped the off-bail on its way through to Frankie who caught the bail instead of the ball and held it up in the air with a loud appeal.

"Good job he didn't get an edge," said Marty as he went to retrieve the ball.

"We'll have to bowl them out," said Cal to me. "No one's going to take a catch today."

The very next moment he was lying across the pitch having just failed to hold a difficult caught and bowled. It began to look as if it wasn't going to be our day.

Next over Tylan bowled another short one which Dave Bickerton swung at. He got a thick top edge which went high to mid-wicket and Erica of all people spilled another chance. She's usually got the safest pair of hands in the team, and she ran in well and got in perfect position to take the catch, but she must have just taken her eyes off it at the last moment. She was furious with herself.

Ten overs gone and they were strolling it – or rather, we were handing it to them. Cal had two close appeals for lbw and another catch went down behind the stumps off Tylan. This time it was a really difficult one – a thick edge which Frankie did well to get a glove on. But it fell to the ground like all the others.

I don't believe it, that's six chances, I thought – but I didn't say anything in case I was next to drop one.

The fifty came in Tylan's last over and the next ball was struck hard and low by Dave Bickerton to mid-on. The ball never rose more than a foot off the ground and seeing who it was fielding there we were all looking towards the boundary for four runs. That was when Ohbert stuck out a hand and held an astonishing catch. For a second no one moved. The batsman and Tylan both stared at Ohbert in disbelief.

As usual Frankie broke the silence. "Don't just stand there, Ohbert," he said. "Chuck the ball in and let's get on with the game."

Tylan rushed over to Ohbert and slapped him on the back, "Outrageous," he said. "But don't keep it a secret – tell everyone how you do it."

"Oh but . . . " said Ohbert. "I didn't see it really."

"Best way," said Cal.

"Perhaps I'll give it a try," said Frankie. "What do you do, Ohbert? Shut your eyes?"

To be fair, Ohbert's got a pretty good record of taking brilliant catches – it's just the way he does it. And, of course, he always misses the easy ones.

Two balls later, with the last ball of his spell, Tylan trapped the incoming batsman lbw – a low full toss hit him on the foot dead in front of his stumps.

50 for four with six overs remaining. I threw the ball to Cal. "Come on," I said, "they need 24 off six. We can still do it."

"Only one problem," said Cal. "I've bowled my four overs."

He had. And so had Tylan. The rule in twenty overs cricket is that no bowler can bowl more than four overs and I'd completely forgotten to keep count. I took the ball and marked out my run as if nothing had happened. Who should I bring on at the other end? Clive or Erica? I decided to go for Erica.

I bowl left armed, over the wicket, a shade slower than Marty or Jacky. My natural ball goes across the right-handed batsman and I often get outside edges to the slips. But could I risk a slip today with so few runs to play with? I decided not.

Of course, my second ball flew off an outside edge to where slip would have been for a single. Then the new batsman connected with a big swing which went just over Tylan's head at square-leg.

Erica came on and Clive scowled at me. There was no doubt he thought he should be bowling – but who cared? I'd had enough of Clive for one day. Fortunately Erica bowled really well – her first over went for only two runs.

Then I got one to pitch on off-stump and nip back between bat and pad. Over went the off-stump. It was a classic left-arm delivery.

In came Seager, the other opening bowler. You could see straightaway from the way he held the bat he was a real slogger. He hammered my first ball to mid-wicket and ran a single.

The first two balls of Erica's next over were snicked in the air through the vacant slip area down to Azzie at third-man. Then Seager connected with a massive heave which dropped just short of a six and bounced over the deep mid-wicket boundary. Two more wild swings missed completely and the last ball of the over grazed the off-stump but the bails stayed.

They now needed only seven off two overs. If we keep it really tight, I thought, we can still win this. And we badly needed a win – it would make all the difference to everyone's confidence. Think of it – played one, won one.

I tried to concentrate really hard. Cal had the same idea. "Come on everyone, let's cut out those singles," he shouted.

I brought in the field a bit closer but they still managed to run a leg-bye to Ohbert. That brought the slogger to face my

This is for all left-handers. To make the ball cut in you hold the ball like this and as you release it the second finger pulls the ball down in an anti-clockwise direction. You feel as if you're pushing the ball towards slip with your thumb. The perfect ball will be pitched just on middle-and-off or off-stump.

bowling. He missed with a great heave and was nearly stumped as Frankie threw down the wicket. Then a thick edge behind square on the off-side brought two runs. I bowled the next one into his pads and he swung and missed but he managed to kick the ball down the leg side. I appealed for lbw.

"Not Out," said Sid and they ran two leg-byes. Another edge lobbed just over cover-point for a single and the scores were level. I changed to bowling round the wicket for my last ball and clean bowled him. The stumps went flying.

But it was too late. The scores were level – they needed only one to win and there were still six balls to bowl. Why hadn't I tried bowling round the wicket earlier?

The first ball of Erica's over was a beauty. It lifted and caught the slogger's glove and lobbed into Frankie's hands. Could we still do it?

No. Two balls later the batsman scurried through for a quick single and they'd won with three balls to spare.

"Hard luck, Hooker," said Cal coming over to me. "If only we'd held our catches."

If only.

INNINGS OF BARMEWELL | TOSS WON BY BARM. | WEATHER FINE

BATSMAN	RUNS SCORED	HOW OUT	BOWLER	SCORE
1 B.SILVER	2.1.1.1.1 >>	bowled	SEBASTIEN	6
2 D.BICKERTON	3.4.1.1.2.1.2.1.1.1.2.1.1.1.2 >>	ct BENNETT	VELLACOTT	24
3 C.EGBUNIKE	1.4 >>	bowled	VELLACOTT	5
4 B.MAYER	2.2.1.1.2.1.1.1 >>	bowled	KNIGHT	12
5 B.BINLEY	>>	lbw	VELLACOTT	0
6 J.ROWELL	3.1.1 >>	bowled	KNIGHT	5
7 A.SEAGER	1.2.2.4.2.1 >>	ct ALLEN	DAVIES	12
8 P.MURRAY		NOT	OUT	0
9 R.MACPHEE	1.	NOT	OUT	1
10				
11				

FALL OF WICKETS

SCORE	25	31	50	50	58	73	73	8	9	10
	1	2	3	4	5	6	7			
BAT NO	1	3	2	5	4	7	6			

		TOTAL
BYES	2	2
L BYES	1.1.2	4
WIDES	1.1.1	3
NO BALLS		

TOTAL EXTRAS 9
TOTAL 74
FOR WKTS 7

SCORE AT A GLANCE

BOWLING ANALYSIS ⊙ NO BALL + WIDE

BOWLER	1	2	3	4	5	6	7	8	9	10	11	12	13	OVS	MDS	RUNS	WKT
1 M.LEAR	M.	4.	..2	X										3	1	9	0
2 J.GUNN	.2	..2.	2.1	X										3	0	14	0
3 C.SEBASTIEN	⊙W.	..1	..2	1.1	X									4	0	10	1
4 T.VELLACOTT	+4.	..1	..1	1.2										4	0	15	3
5 H.KNIGHT	.1	..1	..2											3	0	9	2
6 E.DAVIES	..	22.	W.1											2.3	0	11	1
7																	
8																	
9																	

Chapter Three

For some of us – like Cal, Azzie, Marty and me – Glory
Gardens isn't just a cricket team, it's more a way of life.
We watch cricket, read about cricket, play cricket and everything else just gets in the way of cricket. It's all Cal and I talk
about whenever we get the chance – and that's quite often
because he lives next door.

None of the others are quite so obsessed. Clive's a brilliant
cricketer but it all comes so easily for him that you sometimes
think he doesn't care. And he only likes playing proper games;
he hates Nets. Jason's not as keen as he used to be since he got
interested in chess. Frankie doesn't take anything seriously.
Jacky's really competitive but he's keen on all sports and I
think he prefers football. Tylan's got lots of other interests,
too – like drawing and photography. Matt doesn't say much.
Erica's not the obsessive type – she's too sensible. And that
leaves Ohbert, and who knows what Ohbert thinks.

But when it comes to fanatical support for Glory Gardens,
no one beats Jo.

As you know, Jo is the Club Secretary as well as our scorer; it's her job to look after things like meetings and fixtures.
She's brilliant at it because she's so efficient and tidy and
organised – which makes it doubly strange that she is
Frankie's sister because he's a complete mess.

The day after the game, Jo called an 'Extraordinary Meeting of Glory Gardens Cricket Club'. Kiddo said we could use
his classroom after school, as long as we were out by 5

o'clock when the cleaners come in.

When we arrived we found Jo had put a brown envelope on every desk, each with a name typed on it.

"Please sit down at the desk with your envelope on it,' said Jo. "And don't open it until I tell you, Francis."

Frankie was holding his envelope up to the light. "Must be our pay cheques," he said. "I wonder how much we get per match."

"We ought to charge you 50p for every catch you drop," said Tylan. "We'd make a fortune by the end of the season."

Frankie aimed a kick at him.

We had to hang around for Matthew, Jacky and Clive to arrive because they all go to different schools. The first two soon turned up but as usual Clive was late. We waited another ten minutes then Jo decided to start the meeting without him.

"I've called this meeting," said Jo, "because I think Glory Gardens can win the League." She looked at us one by one. "I take it you all agree with that?"

"Yes," we all said feebly except Frankie who said, "Yes, Miss," and Marty who said nothing.

"Okay then, open your envelopes and look at the top sheet of paper only."

"This is worse than school," said Frankie. "At least you can go to sleep in lessons." Jo didn't hear – or pretended not to.

There were two sheets of paper in the envelope. The first had the results of last night's League games.

NORTH COUNTY UNDER 13 LEAGUE

Glory Gardens *lost to* Barmewell by three wickets
Old Courtiers *beat* Mudlarks by 20 runs
Wyckham Wanderers *beat* Grunty Dyke by two wickets
League positions:

Barmewell	10	Glory Gardens	0
Old Courtiers	10	Grunty Dyke	0
Wyckham Wanderers	10	Mudlarks	0

"We're fourth!" said Ohbert.

"You could say that," said Cal. "Sounds better than equal bottom."

"It's not a great start," said Jo.

"Particularly when Barmewell's supposed to be one of the weakest teams," I said.

"They were good," said Jacky.

"But barmy," said Tylan.

"Not as good as Mudlarks and Wyckham," said Cal. "And Kiddo says Old Courtiers are the best of the lot. Anyway, we should have won. That's 10 points thrown away."

"I have a question," said Frankie. "Who are Grunty Dyke?"

Tylan and Jason sniggered.

"I mean it can't be a cricket team, can it?" said Frankie. "Sounds more like a pig farm."

"Cut it out, Francis. If you must know it's a village team. The village is called Grunty Dyke." Jo looked round sternly to make sure everyone was happy with her explanation. Then she said, "Right if you all turn over the sheet you'll find the fixtures for the League."

We obeyed.

NORTH COUNTY UNDER 13 LEAGUE

Fixtures:
(all matches start at 5pm unless otherwise stated)

Thursday 5th May
Glory Gardens v Barmewell
Old Courtiers v Mudlarks
Wyckham Wanderers v Grunty Dyke

Thursday 12th May
Mudlarks v Glory Gardens
Barmewell v Wyckham Wanderers
Grunty Dyke v Old Courtiers

Thursday 19th May
Grunty Dyke v Glory Gardens

Wyckham Wanderers v Old Courtiers
Mudlarks v Barmewell

Thursday 26th May
Glory Gardens v Wyckham Wanderers
Old Courtiers v Barmewell
Grunty Dyke v Mudlarks

Thursday 9th June
Glory Gardens v Old Courtiers
Wyckham Wanderers v Mudlarks
Barmewell v Grunty Dyke

"Mudlarks next," said Marty. "That'll be a really tough game." Mudlarks had beaten us in the Cup Final last year. Marty would never forget it. We lost off the last ball of the game when he hit his wicket going for the winning runs.

"'Spect their Under Thirteen side will be even stronger," he added glumly.

"Then it's off to Grunty Dyke," said Frankie. "I wonder what their ground's like. We'll probably be changing in a pig sty."

"With your bedroom you'll be used to that," said Jo.

At that moment Clive walked in followed by Kiddo.

"Your stupid caretaker threw me out," said Clive angrily as we all pounced on him for being late.

"It's lucky I was there," said Kiddo. "Bernie was about to eject him from the premises." He looked around. "Well, I won't disturb your meeting, kiddoes. It was a good game on Wednesday by the way. But maybe we should try some catching practice at Nets tomorrow." And with a smile, he left.

"I'm surprised he didn't say 'Catches win matches'," said Cal.

"He will," said Frankie. "Bet you 50p he says it tomorrow at Nets."

Jo called the meeting to order again and told us to look at the second bit of paper which was about 'Elections'. That didn't take long because we just agreed to keep everything the same. So the selection committee was still the Captain, Vice–captain and Secretary. In others words me, Marty and Jo.

We also voted Matthew in as Treasurer again and he gave the 'Treasurer's Report'. He told us that we had £95.20 in our Post Office Giro Account.

"We're the richest club in the League, even if we're not the best," said Tylan.

"Perhaps we should buy some new players," said Frankie.

"Starting with a wicket–keeper," said Cal.

The reason we had so much money was because of Tylan's dad's market stall. Last summer we'd agreed to take turns working on the stall on Saturday mornings so that Tylan could come to Nets. His old man had to have some help on the stall on Saturdays and he couldn't afford to pay anyone properly. So Tylan got stuck with working every Saturday until Erica came up with the idea of taking turns.

Tylan's dad's all right really. He lets us keep the tips and now and again he gives us a couple of quid for the Club. All the money goes into the Glory Gardens Giro Account.

Everyone gets free underwear, too, because that's what Mr Vellacott sells. His stall specialises in knickers and underpants and that sort of thing. We'd done the 'Knicker Rota' right through the winter and that's why we've got nearly a hundred pounds. Ohbert's the star of the stall. He always earns the most money and Mr V says he sells more knickers when Ohbert's on the Rota than with the rest of us put together.

"What kit do we need?" asked Jo.

"A pair of batting gloves," said Cal.

"And some wicket–keeper's gloves," said Frankie. "I can hardly get my hands in the old ones. That's probably why I dropped those two catches."

"Can we afford a pair of specs and lessons from Steve

33

Rhodes, too?" asked Cal.

Frankie said, "I'll give you 50p for every catch I drop if you'll pay me 50p for each one I catch."

"Put it there," said Cal grabbing Frankie's hand.

"Me, too," said Tylan and Azzie. But Frankie wasn't taking any more bets.

"Okay, now turn over the second sheet of paper," said Jo. We looked and read.

TEN THINGS TO HELP GLORY GARDENS WIN THE LEAGUE

1 URGENT. Improve our catching and throwing.
2 Francis needs lots of wicket–keeping practice (and he should lose some weight).
3 Too many batsmen are throwing away their wickets especially Francis but also Cal, Hooker, Azzie and Clive.
4 The 'tail–enders' aren't getting enough serious batting practice.
5 We should be a lot keener in the field.
6 There's too much grumbling about other players. (You know who I'm talking about.)
7 Ask Kiddo to do more video recording in Nets. (I'll do it if you like.)
8 We don't look very smart.
9 We need a couple more players in the Club in case people are ill.
10 Unless we all believe we're going to win the League, we won't.

"She gets worse and worse," said Frankie.

"But she's right," said Cal. "We may be the youngest team in the League, but we're good enough to beat any of them."

"Except the Barmies," said Frankie. "We've already blown that one."

"Well, I think it's all rubbish!" said Clive suddenly.

"You would!" said Jacky. "So let's hear what you'd do."

34

"Well, I agree about finding some better players," said Clive. "But practice isn't the answer. There are some people in this team who wouldn't be cricketers if they practised all day."

"Name them!" said Jason.

"Oh shut up, all of you." I'd had enough of the arguing and squabbling. "I suggest we vote on Jo's plan and if we agree with her, then we start to do something about it at Nets tomorrow. All those in favour."

Everyone put up their hands except Clive and Frankie.

Frankie grinned, "I can't agree with that bit about me being too fat. Well, it's sizist for a start."

"And true," said Cal. "We'll be giving you a free transfer to Grunty Dyke if you get any bigger."

"And what's this about not being smart?" asked Frankie. "Who does she mean?"

"She means your red socks for a start," said Jo. "You can't play cricket in red socks."

"And Tylan's black trainers," said Erica.

"And Ohbert's baseball caps," said Azzie.

Everyone looked at Ohbert. He was asleep – his mouth wide open. A low buzz was coming from his Walkman which he was wearing over his baseball cap, the green and yellow one.

"Why do I bother?" said Jo sadly.

Chapter Four

"**R**ight, kiddoes. Catches win matches. Time for some practice."

Frankie held his hand out to Cal. "50p. Put it there."

"Don't be crazy," said Cal. "I didn't bet you that."

"Yes you did," said Frankie. "I've got witnesses."

"Who?"

Frankie turned to Tylan and Jacky but they both shrugged and said nothing.

"I've only got one bet with you," insisted Cal. "50p for every catch you drop behind the wicket. I can't wait to make my fortune."

Net practice is at the Priory ground every Saturday morning. 10 o'clock start. There are three grass nets and there's a slip catcher and even a bowling machine – but we haven't had a go with that yet.

Kiddo split us into two groups. Azzie, Cal and Matthew worked on the slip catcher with Dave Wing from the Priory First Team. The rest of us: me, Jason, Erica, Frankie, Tylan, Jacky and Ohbert practised high catches. Marty was on the Knicker Rota and Clive hadn't turned up yet. Surprise surprise!

Kiddo lined us up in front of him with Frankie to his right behind the stumps. Then, holding his bat one-handed, he belted the ball as high as he could up in the air. We took turns to run in and catch it and throw it back over the stumps to Frankie.

Kiddo watched us for a bit and then reminded us of the two different ways of taking a high catch.

He said it didn't matter which one we chose – whichever felt the more natural. But once we'd decided on one, we should stick to it and practise it hard. The main thing is to move into line as soon as you've sighted the ball and steady yourself before it arrives. Try and take the catch high before the ball has passed your eyes. That way you can watch it into your hands. Another tip is not to worry about the ball hurting your hands. "If you catch it properly it doesn't hurt," – so Kiddo says.

Ohbert didn't catch a single ball and most of his throws to Frankie ended up further away from the stumps than they started.

"He's saving up his catches for League games," said Frankie. "No point in wasting them at practice, is there, Ohbert?"

The normal 'cupped' technique – Jacky.

And the 'baseball' method – Erica.

"Oh but, they're so high. There's too long to think about what to do," said Ohbert.

"Try closing your eyes until the last minute," said Tylan. It was a dangerous thing to suggest to Ohbert because that's just what he did. He ran straight into Jason with his eyes tight shut.

Next Kiddo lined us up in a semi-circle about 10 metres away from him. Jacky threw the ball to him and he knocked catches to us.

Jacky and Erica were best at catching balls at chest or head height – the kind of catch you often get in the covers or mid-wicket. That's the sort of thing you have to try and remember when you're captain. A lot of field placing ideas can be picked up in practice.

We were just starting batting and bowling in the nets when Clive turned up. He mumbled something about oversleeping and slouched over to the kit bag to put his pads on.

"I knew he'd come," said Cal to me. "He's frightened of the Wrath of Jo."

Clive doesn't have much time for net practice. Don't get me wrong he loves playing cricket, but he says Nets are boring. Maybe he just thinks he's too good to need to practise. However, he knows Jo has a 'Club Rule' – if you don't come to Nets you're out of the team. Clive was dropped once last year for just that reason. So I was glad he'd showed up because we needed him in the side. Sometimes, though, he's more trouble than he's worth. He's never really fitted in with the rest of the team. It's almost as if he enjoys being a loner.

Cal and I joined Jacky, Tylan and Erica for bowling practice with Dave Wing. He opens the bowling for the Priory First XI and he's really quick. He plays in the Minor Counties League sometimes, too, when he can get the time off from work.

Wingy's a brilliant coach and he can bowl spin as well as fast stuff. He talked to Cal and Tylan for a long time about their grip and bowling action.

Off-break grip.

Leg break grip.

Cal bowls an off-break. He stands tall with his left leg braced. His left shoulder should point down the wicket as he reaches the crease. Cal has big hands and can manage the off-break grip. The first and second fingers are spread wide along the seam; it's the first finger that does the spinning.

The grip for Tylan's leg break is completely different. The ball is held by the first three fingers only with the thumb just resting on the seam. The third finger is the main spinning finger.

Tylan had been watching Shane Warne and wanted to learn how to bowl a googly. Wingy told him he'd teach him that when he could really bowl the leg break well without two or three loose balls an over. The secret with the leg break is to keep the wrist bent inwards so that it can twist and flip towards the batsman at the moment of delivery. It just takes loads of practice to get it right.

Tylan told us he was going to learn the googly whatever Wingy said. "I'll ask Azzie's dad – he'll know the secret."

"What exactly is a googly?" asked Erica.

"Glad you asked," said Cal.

"Well, it looks like a leg break, but instead of spinning from leg to off to a right-hand batsman it goes the other way and spins into him. It's a sort of surprise ball." Tylan was waving his arms about showing the ball darting right to left and then left to right.

"Sounds a bit technical to me," said Cal. "Maybe Wingy's right – you know how easily you get confused, Ty."

The last part of Nets was a five pairs game. We split up into five teams of two. Each pair bats for four overs and then takes turns to bowl and field like this.

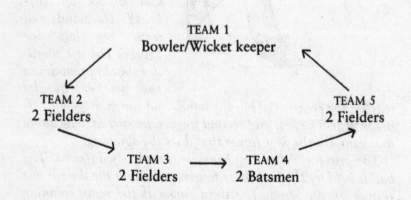

TEAM 1
Bowler/Wicket keeper

TEAM 2
2 Fielders

TEAM 5
2 Fielders

TEAM 3
2 Fielders

TEAM 4
2 Batsmen

Jo scored and Kiddo umpired. You play exactly as in softball cricket – except you're in pairs instead of teams of eight. Runs are scored just like in ordinary cricket except you start with 100 runs and eight runs are taken off your score each time you're out. Each team carries on batting for four overs – no matter how many times they are out. Then the next team bats, and so on.

Clive got the hump because he was paired with Ohbert who kept losing all their runs by getting out. He was out nine times in all. Finally Clive got so angry with Ohbert he didn't see Gatting waddling across the pitch as he was going for a second run and he fell over him and was run out by Jacky. To make things worse, Gatting gave him a great smelly lick.

Everyone laughed, but I think some people (Jacky and Jason, for example) thought it was extra-funny because it was Clive. You couldn't blame them. Clive was always making sneaky comments to them about 'people who couldn't play cricket'. He was rude about Frankie and Ohbert, too – but they didn't seem to notice.

Clive's arrogant. He can't help it – it's just the way he is. Mind you, he hasn't had it easy. His mum died in a car crash when he was about seven and ever since his old man's been a disaster. You sometimes see him staggering around town with a can of beer in his hand shouting and swearing at the shoppers. And last year he threw a brick through the Priory pavilion window.

In the end things got so bad Clive ran away from home. He's living with his aunt now and she's great. She often comes along to cricket and brings us cakes and home-made biscuits. Clive's got a lot better since he's been living with her but he still says some pretty horrible things sometimes. And he hates people laughing at him.

Later, when Jacky was batting, Clive deliberately tripped him up. He pretended he was fielding a ball but everyone could see it was a deliberate trip. Jacky over-reacted and threw his bat at Clive. It caught him on the shoulder.

Kiddo and Cal grabbed them before anything serious happened. Even so, Clive tried to swing a punch at Jacky but it hit Cal on the arm instead. Kiddo took them both to one side and gave them one of his lectures.

"You can't blame Jacky," said Tylan. "Clive always goes too far."

"Yeah," said Jason. "It's time someone sorted him out."

"Time we got on with the game," said Cal.

In the end Erica and Azzie won with a score of 124 – they didn't lose any wickets. Tylan and I got 120 but it would have been 136 if we hadn't got out once each. Clive and Ohbert were last with 39.

———— • ————

Cal and I walked home together after Nets.

"That's the last time I do that," said Cal.

"What?"

"Break up a fight. All you get for it is a big bruise on the arm."

I told Cal I was getting worried about the row between Clive and Jacky. "It's starting to get to the rest of the team."

"Yeah, Clive's going through one of his strange periods," said Cal. "I suppose he'll get over it."

"Most captains don't have a problem like this," I said. "What am I doing wrong?"

"Most captains don't have to deal with people like Clive."

"Bet they do. Bet you there's a Clive and a Frankie and an Ohbert in nearly every team."

"What a horrible thought," said Cal with a big grin. "All those Ohberts!"

"Clive upsets people," I said. "And Jacky can't take it. It's messing up his bowling, too. Look at the way he bowled against Barmewell."

"Well, you could drop Clive," said Cal.

"Do you think we should?"

"Dunno."

"You're a great help," I said.

We went to Cal's for lunch because my sister had some of her friends round at my house. We spent most of the afternoon working out the tactics for the Mudlarks game. Then Frankie and Tylan turned up and we went and played cricket on Glory Gardens Rec.

Chapter Five

For away games, we usually go in Kiddo's Volvo Estate and Azzie's dad's Renault Espace. Mudlarks' ground is on the other side of town, not far from where Clive lives, so he came on his own and, for once, he wasn't late.

Everyone was available for the game which meant Ohbert was twelfth man. As usual, Jo wasn't too pleased about dropping him but Marty and I both thought we needed our strongest team out against Mudlarks.

I only recognised four of the players from the team we'd played in the famous Cup Final last year. There was Sam Keeping, their brilliant wicket-keeper – he'd been the captain – the two fast bowlers, Woolf and D'Anger, and Henry Rossi who'd scored 38 against us. The rest of them were 'proper' under 13s and, like the Barmies, a year older than us. They had a new captain, too; his name was Alvin Thomas.

"They've grown fast in a year, haven't they, Ohbert?" said Frankie.

"Oh, but . . . have we played them before, then?" asked Ohbert, adjusting his Walkman. Ohbert had come along to support us even though he wasn't playing. He was wearing baggy orange and pink checked shorts and a horrible slimy green tee-shirt. His Walkman sat on top of a bright blue baseball cap. I thought it must be almost as strange inside Ohbert's wardrobe as it is inside his mind.

It had rained in the week and the pitch was a bit soft but I still decided to bat when I won the toss. Alvin Thomas told me the wicket might be on the slow side but it was usually a good batting track.

Matthew and Cal opened the batting as usual – followed by our strongest middle order: Azzie, Clive, Erica and me at six.

The first ball was bowled spot on five o'clock by Barry Woolf.

We'd scored 10 when the first wicket fell. Matthew wasn't as comfortable as usual, particularly against Woolf who looked a yard quicker than last year. Matt went for a big drive outside the off-stump. He missed and was brilliantly stumped by Sam Keeping who stands up even to the fast bowlers.

"What's got into you?" Frankie asked Matthew when he arrived back. "A bit of a wild shot for Matthew, wasn't it?"

"Oh, I dunno," said Matthew. "I wasn't feeling right today."

I just hoped all the criticism about slow scoring wasn't getting to him.

Azzie took guard and survived a loud lbw appeal off his first ball – it must have been close but it was probably going down the leg side.

Slowly but surely Azzie began to get on top of the bowling. In the next over from Woolf he played his favourite shot – a wonderful cover drive on the front foot. It went for four between cover-point and extra-cover before either of the fielders could move.

Cal played the supporting role perfectly, giving Azzie the strike when he could but also scoring well off the bad balls. The 50 came up in the tenth over and Azzie had scored 31 of them. He was getting his runs with strokes all round the wicket and Alvin was having no end of trouble setting a field for him.

"Look at that!" gasped Jason as a fierce pull off a short ball sped to the boundary. "Azzie's the best!"

"No doubt about it," said Jacky with a pointed look across at Clive. "Best batsman in the League. Don't you agree, Clive?"

The cover drive is played to an over-pitched ball, well outside the off-stump. Azzie brings his front foot to just inside the line of the ball and as he connects on the half-volley, he opens the face of the bat slightly directing the ball in front of square. The full follow through leaves the hand finishing high and, as always, eyes following the direction of the ball.

Clive said nothing. He had a faraway look in his eyes and you could tell he was concentrating hard on what he would do when his turn came.

It wasn't too long coming. Cal played a good hook for four but two balls later he tried to play the same shot to a straighter, fuller ball and top-edged to square-leg.

Clive got up and strolled out to the middle.

"Now let's see what the World's Greatest Batsman can do," said Jacky.

"Azzie needs 13 for his 50," said Jo.

"Six overs to go," said Tylan. "No trouble."

But for the next three overs Azzie didn't face a single ball. Clive's innings grew rapidly in twos and fours – the twos run quickly with Clive calling Azzie through sharply for the second run. But somehow there was never more than a single to be had off the last ball of the over.

On one occasion, he very nearly ran Azzie out, sending him back when there was an easy second run. Azzie was three quarters of the way down the track and he stared in disbelief when Clive refused to run. He turned and only just made it back but if the bowler had been properly positioned behind the stumps he'd have had no chance. It was so close that, if it had been a Test Match, they'd have definitely called in the third umpire.

Clive was hogging the bowling – that was obvious. Okay, he was playing brilliantly, perhaps as well as Azzie, but I got the feeling that was just what Clive was out to prove.

"It's just jealousy," said Jason. "He can't bear anyone thinking Azzie's better than he is."

"Come on, Clive. Give the little master a go," shouted Frankie.

Clive had scored 16 without Azzie facing a single ball.

It was again the last ball of the over.

"Just watch, he'll go for another single," said Jacky.

He was right – Clive pushed the ball to backward square-leg and called for a run. The throw came in wild and way over the keeper's head, there was an easy overthrow. Azzie didn't hesitate; he turned and ran.

"No," shouted Clive.

"Yes," shouted Azzie.

"Run," screamed the whole Glory Gardens team.

Azzie was through for the second run and Clive was forced to jog down to the other end and give up the strike.

Jacky and Matthew were furious. "He'd rather run Azzie out than let him score 50," said Jacky.

Azzie was trying hard to regain his concentration. He'd not faced a ball for so long it was almost like starting his innings all over again. But a straight lofted drive for four soon had him back on course again and he even managed a single from the last ball of the over to keep the strike and give Clive a taste of his own medicine.

But Azzie's too good a team player to worry about getting his own back. A single off the first ball of the over meant that Clive was facing again. And, to prove he could do anything Azzie could, Clive immediately unleashed a drive straight over the bowler's head for four. He looked over his shoulder at us as if to say, 'Beat that.'

The next ball was pitched up even further and Clive stepped down the wicket to play the same shot – but this time he overstretched and turned the ball into a yorker.

He turned and stared in dismay at his off-stump which lay flat on the ground. A cheer went up from the Mudlark players and from at least one or two of the Glory Gardens supporters, too. Clive looked up, stared at us and then took a swing at the remains of the wicket with his bat. The stumps went flying.

"Oh, he's really done it now!" said Cal.

Kiddo was up off his seat in a flash. He stormed out to meet Clive who was making his way slowly back from the middle. Everyone watched as they stood and faced each other. Kiddo furious, hands on hips; Clive slouching, leaning on his bat. The players on the pitch stood and stared at them, too.

Finally, Kiddo and Clive walked together towards old Sid who was standing over the wreckage of the wicket. Clive picked up the stumps and, one by one, replaced them in the ground. Then he put the bails on, spoke briefly to old Sid and walked back to the pavilion with Kiddo. As they passed us Clive refused to look at anyone. He stared straight ahead and walked on to the changing room.

"Brilliant performance," said Frankie applauding him. "Deserves an Oscar."

"Outrageous," said Tylan.

"What are you waiting for?" said Kiddo. "Get on with it."

Erica jumped up and went out to bat.

After all the excitement I had to ask Jo to remind me of the score.

91 for two. Azzie's got 45. Eight balls left of the innings.

The important thing was for Erica to give Azzie the strike. She did just that with her first ball – a quick single run down through the vacant slips. Azzie played a cover drive for two off the last ball of the over but that meant Erica was facing again.

It was a run a ball for the next five balls. Erica was doing just what was needed to put Azzie on strike but Azzie couldn't get the ball past the in-field. Slowly his score crept up. 47 . . . 48 . . . 49 . . .

It was the last ball of the innings, Azzie needed one for his fifty. The ball was bowled just outside the off-stump and Azzie stepped back and forced it to the left of cover-point for four.

Everyone cheered and clapped, including the Mudlarks. It was a great end to a beautiful innings. He hadn't given a single chance. Even Ohbert was clapping; he'd actually taken off his Walkman to watch the end of Azzie's innings.

"Oh, but . . . I wish I could score 50," he said.

Tylan laughed and threw Ohbert's baseball cap up in the air. Cal caught it and threw it up a tree.

"Pity Clive isn't here to clap him in," said Jacky sarcastically. Clive hadn't re-emerged from the changing room.

And as Azzie walked off to the applause of both teams, Frankie put his hand on a bee.

HOME TEAM MUDLARKS	V GLORY GARDENS AWAY TEAM	AT MUDLARKS DATE MAY 12TH

INNINGS OF GLORY GARDENS   **TOSS WON BY** G.G.   **WEATHER** CLOUDY

BATSMAN	RUNS SCORED	HOW OUT	BOWLER	SCORE
1 M. ROSE	1·2·1 ≫	st KEEPING	WOOLF	4
2 C. SEBASTIEN	2·1·1·2·1·1·2·4 ≫	ct WHITE	BRONSTEIN	14
3 A. NAZAR	2·1·1·1·4·2·1·1·2·2·1·4·1·1·4·3·2·4 4·2·1(44)·1·2·1·1·4	NOT	OUT	53
4 C. DA COSTA	1·2·2·1·2·4·2·2·2·4 ≫	bowled	SLYMAN	22
5 E. DAVIES	1·1·1·	NOT	OUT	4
6				
7				
8				
9				
10				
11				

FALL OF WICKETS

	1	2	3	4	5	6	7	8	9	10
SCORE	10	60	91							
BAT NO	1	2	4							

			TOTAL
BYES	1·	1	EXTRAS 6
L.BYES	1·1	2	TOTAL 103
WIDES	1·1	2	FOR
NO BALLS		1	WKTS 3

SCORE AT A GLANCE

BOWLER	BOWLING ANALYSIS ⊙ NO BALL + WIDE													OVS	MDS	RUNS	WKT
	1	2	3	4	5	6	7	8	9	10	11	12	13				
1 B. WOOLF	··· 1·2	··· 2·1	W·2 ··1	·4· 2·1	✕									4	0	16	1
2 A. THOMAS	+·1· ···	M·1·	⊙1· 1··	·1· 2··	✕									4	1	9	0
3 H. ROSSI	·2· 2·1·1	·1· 2··	··2 ·4·	2·· 2·1	✕									4	0	20	0
4 A. D'ANGER	··1 4··1	·4· ·3·	✕											2	0	14	0
5 T. BRONSTEIN	·4· W·1	·2· 4··	·4· 2·1	111 114										4	0	27	1
6 P. SLYMAN	··2 2·2	1·4 W12												2	0	14	1
7																	
8																	
9																	

Chapter Six

"**O**oow ARGGGHH!"

Frankie's scream brought the celebrations to a sudden halt. They must have heard it all over town. He jumped up as if he'd sat on a rattlesnake and ran around waving his hand in the air. I thought, hello, he's finally cracked.

It took some time for us to realise it was a bee sting. But at last Frankie calmed down a bit and Kiddo took him to his car and put something on it from his first-aid kit. The bee had got him in the middle of the palm of his right hand and it had swollen up quickly. It was obvious he wasn't going to be able to keep wicket, although he insisted he could field.

"I'll keep, if you like," suggested Cal.

"No, I want you to bowl," I said. "What do you think about Azzie? He's our best slip fielder."

"Good idea," said Cal. "If he's not too knackered after his 50."

Azzie was really pleased. He used his own pads because Frankie's wicket-keeper's pads were too big for him. So were the gloves but he said he could manage with them.

In the panic over Frankie and the bee sting, no one had spoken to Clive. He sat on his own in complete silence in the corner of the changing room. Normally, Frankie would have said something stupid to him but he was too busy looking at his hand and showing everyone the swelling to think of teasing Clive.

"You'd better speak to him," said Cal to me, nodding in

51

Clive's direction. "You know what he's like. He might go off in a huff."

I wasn't sure I cared. And what could I say to him, anyway? "Don't worry about nearly wrecking Azzie's 50. And as for smashing down the stumps – well, that was a good idea and we're all a hundred percent behind you, Clive mate."

Luckily Azzie beat me to it. "I'd forget it if I were you, Clive. You've said sorry – and that's it."

Clive looked at him long and hard. I couldn't tell what was going through his mind. Did he know he'd batted like a selfish baby? Did he think everyone was against him? (They probably were right now.) Or was he just convinced he was the best and no one else mattered?

At last he spoke. "Okay," he said. Then after a pause, "That was a great 50, by the way."

"Thanks."

Jacky and Matthew exchanged glances but no one said any more for the moment because it was time to go out and field.

Marty opened our attack and took a wicket in the first over. It was an important one, too – Henry Rossi, who'd been their top scorer in the Final last summer. He got a thin edge to a ball just outside off-stump and Azzie took a good catch.

"Makes a change to have a real wicket-keeper," said Cal, loud enough for Frankie to hear.

"You're just born lucky, Calvin Sebastien," said Frankie. "That would have cost you 50p if I'd been keeping."

"To bee or not to bee," said Tylan mysteriously.

Frankie was fielding at third-man where, I thought, he was least likely to get a catch. But for Jacky's first over I brought him up to mid-on and, of course, the batsman immediately hit the ball in the air straight at him. It was going quite fast and Frankie took it in both hands. With a scream he threw it up in the air like a hot potato and caught it in his left hand as it came down.

"Okay, Cal. Let's see your money," he said, blowing furiously on his right hand.

"No chance," said Cal. "The bet's only for catches behind the stumps."

"What! You cheat," Frankie protested.

"Ask Jo," said Cal. "She'll remember what you said."

"Some hope. She only remembers when I'm wrong," said Frankie glumly.

The score was 6 for two. Just the start we needed. Now we had to keep the pressure on them. Sam Keeping joined Alvin Thomas at the wicket. Sam can bat a bit but like most of us he's nervous when he first comes in. I brought the field in for him and tried to make it as hard as possible for him to score. Marty and Jacky kept things tight with some really accurate bowling.

Alvin and Sam battled on and they'd taken the score to 27 when Sam got a shooter from Jacky and was clean bowled.

The opening bowlers both finished their spells and I decided to bring Tylan on at one end and me at the other.

Tylan immediately got the ball to turn quite sharply and he had both batsmen playing and missing. But, as usual, he bowled the occasional rubbish ball which was hit for four.

I surprised the new batsman with a shortish, quicker delivery which he gloved to Azzie who took an easy catch.

"I think you've got a permanent job, Azzie," said Cal.

"And, have you noticed, not a single bye," said Marty, winking at Cal.

Frankie scowled. For once he was speechless.

At the half way stage they were 37 for four – not completely out of it, but we were definitely on top. Their captain started to try and push the scoring along. He hit Tylan for a second four over square-leg to bring up the 50. But Tylan got his own back by bowling the other batsman round his legs with a beaut that must have turned nearly six inches.

I brought Cal up to slip and the new batsman edged the very first ball. It went fast and low and Cal took a spectacular diving catch to his left. Two wickets in two balls. But it was the end of his over.

Only one run came off my third over and I had them both playing and missing. With only six overs to go they still needed 52 to win. Now we really had them on the rack. They wanted 8.5 runs an over.

I thought about bringing Erica on for Tylan, to tighten things up, but he was on a hat trick and it wouldn't be right.

I called the field in as close as I could. You're not allowed to have anyone closer than eleven yards in league cricket – except of course, for the keeper, slips and gully.

Tylan ran up and stopped. He'd lost his run up. He walked back, looked round the field and, at last, he bowled to Alvin Thomas. It pitched short and was going down the leg side. Alvin took an enormous swing at it and Cal ducked at short square-leg. There was a sickening dull thud and cry.

I looked towards the square-leg boundary and then back at the batsman. He'd dropped his bat and he was looking at Azzie. Azzie was lying on the ground motionless.

For a moment no one moved. There was silence round the ground. Cal reacted first. He ran up to Azzie, took one look at him and shouted, "Help, quick!"

We all rushed up to where Azzie lay. He was lying on his side, almost as if he were asleep; his hat was on the ground beside him. I picked it up. I couldn't think what else to do.

"Keep back. Don't touch him," said Cal. Azzie wasn't moving. His eyes were closed and he didn't even seem to be breathing.

"What happened?" I asked.

"The end of the bat caught him on the side of his head," said Cal.

Azzie had gone to take the ball down the leg side and he'd taken the full swing of the bat. It was a wicked blow. There was blood coming from a cut just over his ear.

Kiddo was on the spot in seconds. He'd seen it all from the boundary and realised it was serious.

He took a close look at Azzie. "Who knows how my car phone works?"

"I do," said Cal.

"Go with Sid and call for an ambulance," he said handing his car keys to Cal. "Dial 999 and tell them to come to the Mudlarks Club in Marshland Road. Got it?"

Cal ran off without a reply with old Sid and the Mudlarks umpire in hot pursuit.

Kiddo bent over Azzie who still hadn't moved a muscle. He put his ear to Azzie's mouth and listened. We stood and watched and waited. No one said a word. We hardly dared breathe.

Kiddo gently rolled Azzie over on his back and tilted his head back. He opened his mouth and stuck his finger inside.

"Get back all of you," said Kiddo with a firm but calm voice. "Harry, keep everyone back, will you." Old Gatting, who'd followed Kiddo on to the pitch, sat down at Azzie's feet as if guarding him.

Kiddo pinched Azzie's nose between his thumb and finger, knelt forward and blew into his mouth. He did it again and then again. He felt Azzie's chest with his free hand. Then he continued blowing into his mouth. Every now and again he put his ear to Azzie's mouth and listened. Suddenly Kiddo leaned back and let out a big, low sigh. "Where's that ambulance," he snapped.

No one spoke. And then there was a groan from Azzie and he opened his eyes, "Did I catch it?" he said quietly.

"You caught it all right, kiddo," said Kiddo. "How are you feeling?"

"My head!" said Azzie putting his hand to the bloody spot above his ear. Then he was sick.

"Don't worry, kiddo," said Kiddo, holding Azzie's hand. "You've had a bit of a knock and we're going to get you to hospital to have you checked out."

Azzie's head seemed to have stopped bleeding but his face was as white as Sid's umpire's coat.

Seconds later the ambulance arrived. It drove through the gates and headed for us – straight on to the ground and right across the pitch. Azzie was quickly lifted on to a stretcher. In no time he was inside the ambulance.

"Tell his dad we've gone to St Cuthbert's," said Kiddo and within moments he and Azzie were speeding through the gate and along the road, sirens blaring.

We stood together in the middle of the pitch. Gatting had been left behind. He kept blinking and looking at us one by one as if he were waiting for an explanation. I looked at Azzie's 'Ritchie Richardson' hat which I was still holding.

"His dad'll be here soon," said Marty. "What are we going to tell him?" Azzie's dad had gone back to work after dropping us at the ground. He said he'd be back for the last overs.

"Do you think Azzie's all right?" said Frankie quietly.

"Of course he is," said Erica. "But thank God Kiddo was here to give him mouth-to-mouth."

"I hit him really hard," said Alvin Thomas looking blankly at his bat.

"Don't worry, mate," I said. "It wasn't your fault." I knew he must be feeling terrible.

The game was called off. Azzie's dad arrived minutes after the ambulance had left and, as soon as Sid told him what had happened, he immediately jumped back into his Espace and drove to the hospital.

Sid phoned Tylan's dad and Jacky's mum and they said they'd come and pick everyone up from the ground. Cal, Frankie and I decided we'd go along to the hospital to find out how Azzie was getting on. We got changed in record time, without having a shower and ran to catch a bus. There was a bus stop just outside the ground.

Gatting followed along after us as if he knew where we were going. He was carrying his lead in his mouth.

"We'll have to take him," said Cal. "There probably won't be room in the cars for him anyway. And Kiddo will want to know where he is."

I fixed his lead to his collar and at that moment the bus arrived.

INNINGS OF .. MUDLARKS	TOSS WON BY G.G... WEATHER CLOUDY

BATSMAN	RUNS SCORED	HOW OUT	BOWLER	SCORE
1 H.ROSSI	1.	ct NAZAR	LEAR	1
2 A.THOMAS	1.2.1.2.1.2.2.1.4.1.1.2.2.1.4.1.1	NOT	OUT	29
3 K.RUTTER		ct ALLEN	GUNN	0
4 S.KEEPING	1.2.1.2.1.2	bowled	GUNN	9
5 P.SLYMAN	1.2	ct NAZAR	KNIGHT	3
6 H.SPONNE	1.2	bowled	VELLACOTT	3
7 H.CARLTON		ct SEBASTIEN	VELLACOTT	0
8 T.BRONSTEIN		NOT	OUT	0
9				
10	MATCH ABANDONED			
11				

FALL OF WICKETS

	1	2	3	4	5	6	7	8	9	10
SCORE	2	6	27	37	51	51				
BAT NO	1	3	4	5	6	7				

BYES	—	
L BYES	1.1.1.1.	4
WIDES	1.1	2
NO BALLS	1.	1

TOTAL EXTRAS	7
TOTAL FOR WKTS	52 / 6

SCORE AT A GLANCE

BOWLING ANALYSIS ⊙ NO BALL + WIDE

BOWLER	1	2	3	4	5	6	7	8	9	10	11	12	13	OVS	MDS	RUNS	WKT
1 M.LEAR	..1 1W.	..2 +.1.	+.+. 2.1.	1.. 2.1.	✕									4	0	10	1
2 J.GUNN	.⊙.2 W.12.	1.1 .2.	.22 ...	.2. W.1										4	0	15	2
3 T.VELLACOTT	..4 ..1.	..2 +.2.	.+4. 1WW	.										3.1	0	15	2
4 H.KNIGHT	.1. 2.W1	..1. .2.	..1 ...											3	0	8	1
5																	
6																	
7																	
8																	
9																	

Chapter Seven

As we walked into St Cuthbert's hospital a fat woman in a green uniform stopped us. "Where do you kids think you're going with that dog?"

"We're looking for Azzie," said Frankie.

I told her he'd been brought in by ambulance with a head injury.

"He was wicket-keeping, you see," added Frankie.

"Well, you still can't bring the dog in. No dogs allowed."

"He belongs to our teacher," said Frankie, as if that explained everything.

Gatting walked up to the woman, sat down, lifted a paw to her and put his head on one side as if to say, "Oh, go on. Just this once."

She smiled and took his paw. "You sweet old thing," she said. "I've got a little doggie at home who'd like to meet you." Then she turned to us and her face went stern again. "Right, you can take him into the waiting room but if there are any complaints out you go, immediately." And giving Gatting a gentle pat she said, "You'll be a good boy, won't you?" and bustled off.

In the waiting room we found Kiddo sitting on his own. Gatting waddled up to him and nuzzled his nose into his hand and gave him a huge lick.

"Hello, old boy," said Kiddo with a faint smile. He turned to us. "Asif's having an X-ray to see if he's cracked anything. I think he's fine. His dad's with him." He looked at us and then he added, "He'll be batting again in no time, you'll see."

"Had his heart stopped beating?" asked Frankie.

"No. But he wasn't breathing," said Kiddo. "He swallowed his tongue when he was hit."

"It was a wicked thump," said Frankie. "He was unconscious for ages."

"Seemed like that, kiddo, didn't it," said Kiddo. "But I bet he wasn't out for more than a couple of minutes. You lose all track of time at moments like that."

We waited and waited. It seemed like hours. The fat woman came to check on us and she brought a bowl of water for Gatting. You could see Kiddo didn't think much of Gatting being called a 'sweet old doggie' and 'a thirsty little darling'. He kept raising his eyebrows and looking uncomfortable but I don't think she noticed. Frankie did a good impersonation of the way she walked and Kiddo told him to sit down and read a magazine.

At last Azzie's dad came in. "They think he might have a hairline fracture of the skull," he said. "Anyway, it's not too serious but they're going to keep him in for observation for a couple of days. He'll be okay though. He's looking fine."

"Hurray!" said Frankie. "Can we see him?"

"I don't know, you'll have to ask the doctor."

"I'll find him," said Frankie – and he rushed off before anyone could stop him.

As soon as he'd disappeared, the doctor came in and told us we could have a couple of minutes with Azzie. He was in a little room off a long corridor. We found him sitting up on a sort of bed with wheels wearing a white elastic bandage round his head. He still looked pale and his head seemed swollen on one side but he grinned at us as we walked in.

"Did we win?" he asked.

"No result," said Cal. "You wouldn't expect us to play on after your ambulance had churned up the pitch, would you?"

"That's a shame," said Azzie. "We'd have won easily."

"He wants to know when he'll be able to play cricket

again," said Azzie's dad with a smile to the doctor.

"Oh, two or three weeks if he behaves himself."

"That's no good," said Azzie. "I could always bat with a helmet."

"Don't think you'd get one on," said Cal.

The doctor told us we'd have to leave because Azzie was being moved to his bed in the ward. Just as we were going Frankie bounced in.

"Oh that's where you are," he said. "That woman tried to throw me out but I escaped." He grinned at Azzie. "Hello, Azzie. Still want to be a wicket-keeper?"

"No," said Azzie. "You can keep it – it's too much of a headache."

"That's a shame," said Cal. "Just when we get a proper keeper he goes and resigns. How's the bee sting by the way, Frankie?"

"What sting?" said Frankie. He seemed to have forgotten all about the 'excruciating pain'. Then he held out his right hand. "Oh, yes, perhaps I should have it seen to while I'm here." He showed his hand to the doctor and we all laughed.

Frankie gave Azzie what was left of the bag of sweets he'd been eating all evening. "We'll be back tomorrow night," he said. "Hope the food's good."

———————— ● ————————

At school next day everyone wanted to know about Azzie.

"His skull's cracked down the middle," Frankie told them. "Just shows you how dangerous it is being a wicket-keeper."

"You don't have to worry, your head's too thick to crack," said Jo.

"Thanks," said Frankie. "But I'm not bothered about being hit with a cricket bat. It's having mouth to mouth from Kiddo that worries me."

Erica said we should do a get-well card for Azzie and take it along that evening. "We can make a big card and everyone can put a message on it."

"Or do a drawing?" suggested Tylan, who's the best artist in the school.

Jo had made a 'batogram' of Azzie's great innings and we decided we'd put that on the front of the card.

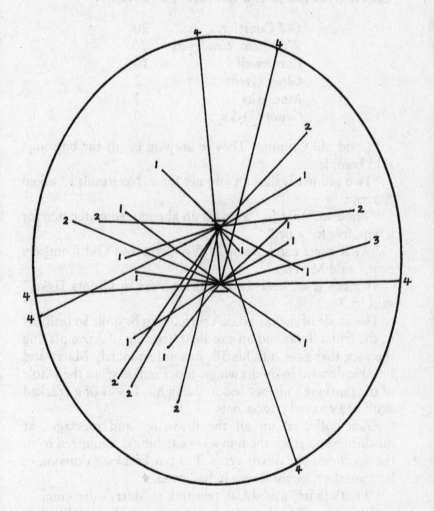

Jo also had the results of the other League games and – worse luck – the League table.

Mudlarks v Glory Gardens no result
Barmewell *lost to* **Wyckham Wanderers by 5 wickets**
Grunty Dyke *lost to* **Old Courtiers by 13 runs**

Old Courtiers	20
Wyckham Wanderers	20
Barmewell	10
Glory Gardens	2
Mudlarks	2
Grunty Dyke	0

"Good old Grunties! They're keeping us off the bottom," said Frankie.

"Two points! Is that all you get for a 'No Result'?" asked Marty.

"'Fraid so," said Jo. "Two for an abandoned match, ten for a win, five for a tie."

"We'll never catch up with Wyckham and Old Courtiers now," said Marty.

"We can if we beat them both and win at Grunty Dyke," said Jo.

The inside of the card didn't turn out to be quite so brilliant as the front. Tylan did an excellent drawing of Azzie playing the shot that gave him his 50. But unfortunately Marty and Frankie decided to do drawings, too. Frankie spent the whole of the morning's history lesson doing his. It was of a cracked skull and crossed cricket bats.

Erica collected up all the drawings and messages at lunchtime and stuck them in a big card she'd scrounged from the art room. She nearly refused to put Frankie's drawing in because she thought it was in bad taste.

"What's that?" asked Cal, pointing at Marty's drawing.

"It's a row of cricket bats hanging upside down – like live bats do when they're asleep," said Marty. "That's why it says watch out for flying bats, see?"

"Oh yeah," said Cal. "Pity it looks like six green bottles falling off a wall."

"More like a load of dead gerbils hanging on a washing line," said Frankie.

"Shut up, Francis. You get more and more disgusting," said Jo. "Look at that drawing you've done. It's sick!"

"You just don't understand about modern art," said Frankie.

———————— • ————————

Azzie was sitting up in bed when we all turned up to see him after school. He thought the card was great – especially the batogram and Frankie's drawing – so Jo and Frankie were both happy.

There were ten of us plus Azzie's mum and brother gathered around the bed; it was a bit crowded.

"Guess who I saw earlier?" said Azzie.

"The brain surgeon?" said Frankie.

"Liam Katz," said Azzie. "He was visiting his grandmother. She's in the next ward and he walked in here by mistake."

Liam was the captain of Wyckham Wanderers, our most deadly enemies. Liam's all right really – except he's a big-head, even if he is the best cricketer in the League. We'd played two games against Wyckham last year and so far we had one win each.

"Suppose he told you they've got a brilliant team this year as usual," said Cal with a pretend yawn.

"Yeah, they've got a bowler who's faster than Win Reifer and a spinner who's the best Liam's ever seen," said Azzie.

"He always was a big mouth," said Frankie.

"Francis, you have a nerve, I'll say that for you," sighed Jo.

"Liam says we should watch out at Grunty Dyke," said Azzie.

"Why?"

"Well it's a lousy pitch, for a start, and they're all cheats. He says two of their batsmen refused to walk for catches behind the wicket. And they appeal every time the ball hits your pads. He says their captain's the worst. His name is Darren Hogg and his dad runs the team and he's just as bad."

"Beware the Hoggs of Grunty Dyke," sniggered Frankie.

"No jokes," begged Cal. "Remember, Azzie's sick."

"No he's not," said Azzie. "They're letting me out tomorrow. They think my brain's all right."

"That bang with the bat must have cured it then," said Frankie.

At that moment Clive walked in. He looked a little surprised to see so many people gathered around Azzie's bed. "I've brought you a present," he said. And he gave Azzie a box of his aunt's best chocolate brownies.

Azzie shared them out and for a while I forgot about the problems of being captain of Glory Gardens.

Then the fat woman came in and said there were too many people round Azzie's bed and we'd have to leave. As we were going she asked me, "How's your dear little doggie?"

"He's under the bed," said Frankie.

And believe it or not, she got down on her hands and knees and crawled under the bed to look for Gatting.

By the time she got up, we'd gone.

Chapter Eight

No Azzie. And now Marty was out, too. He twisted his ankle doing circuit training in P.E. on Wednesday and by Thursday morning he could hardly walk. We'd lost our best batsman and best bowler in less than a week.

We desperately needed another player – or two really, because otherwise we'd have to play Ohbert. There was no one at school who was any good. Acfield Todd who used to play the odd game for us had left at Easter. Jacky Gunn said his brother, Brian, would play if we were really stuck. Brian's thirteen but he just qualifies for the League because his birthday's on September 6th and the rules say you have to be under thirteen on September 1st.

We couldn't find anyone else at such short notice, so the line up for the Grunty Dyke game was a bit different from the team that had played against Mudlarks.

Matthew Rose	Tylan Vellacott
Cal Sebastien	Frankie Allen
Clive da Costa	Brian Gunn
Erica Davies	Jacky Gunn
Hooker Knight	Ohbert Bennett
Jason Padgett	

Kiddo borrowed the school's minibus to take us to Grunty Dyke because it was about six miles out of town and Azzie's dad was busy. He picked up Matthew, Jacky, his brother and

Clive on the way. Of course, Clive wasn't there when we arrived and we had to hang around waiting for him for nearly ten minutes. Kiddo almost left without him. Then we got lost and we spent ages driving around looking for the Grunty Dyke ground.

Frankie made things worse by singing a stupid song with even stupider words. "Didn't we have a lovely time the day we went to Grunty." He sang it over and over until Kiddo told him to 'give it a rest'.

At last we arrived. We were late and Kiddo had steam coming out of his ears.

"So this is Grunty," said Frankie. "Looks more like a ploughed field to me."

"Perhaps they use pigs instead of a lawn mower," said Tylan.

The pitch looked every bit as bad as Liam Katz had said. There was a lot of grass on the wicket and the outfield was rutted and bumpy. Still at least we were here and ready to play. We'd all come changed for the game – so there wouldn't be much of a delay.

As we jumped out of the bus a spotty boy with short fair hair came up to us followed by a red-faced man with a bristly beard.

"Hurry up! We're batting," said the spotty boy who turned out to be Darren Hogg, their captain. He'd already got his pads on.

"What do you mean?" I said. "We haven't tossed yet."

"You've already lost the toss," said the bristly man who was wearing a bright yellow, shiny shellsuit and a yellow baseball cap. He introduced himself as 'Mr Hogg, the team manager and Darren's dad.' And he went on, "The rules state that any team arriving more than fifteen minutes after the appointed starting time shall forfeit the right to win the toss."

"Oh come on, it's only just after quarter past," said Kiddo; you could see he was struggling to control himself. "We got lost. There are no signs to the village, let alone to the ground and the directions we were given were hopeless."

"Sorry," said bristly Hogg. "Rules are rules."

Kiddo shrugged and told us rather gruffly to 'get fielding'.

"Charming pair, the Hoggs," said Erica. "It'll be a pleasure to beat them."

"We'll make mincemeat of them," said Jason.

"You mean sausage meat, don't you?" said Tylan.

Frankie finally emerged from the changing room with his keeper's pads on. He was chuckling to himself.

"The rules state that you shall not speak to my sister as if she's a half-wit who doesn't know anything about cricket," he said in a very Hogg-like voice.

He told us that bristly Hogg was doing the scoring with Jo and he was actually daring to explain the rules to her – to Jo who knew more about scoring than anyone in the League!

"What's worse is that he's getting half of it wrong," said Frankie. "I think Jo'll gouge his eyeballs out with her pencil if he calls her 'little girl' once more."

"Does Brian bowl?" Cal asked Jacky. I realised I didn't even know whether he could play cricket at all. Brian doesn't look anything like Jacky. He's much taller and he has straightish blonde hair and sticking-out ears.

"No chance," said Jacky. "He can bat but he's a slogger."

"Worse than Frankie?" I asked.

"About the same," said Jacky with a shrug.

Darren Hogg opened the batting for the Grunties. He was such a big-head I guessed he'd probably open the bowling, too. The other opener was Phil Thacker, a sour-faced boy with a big nose.

Darren took strike. "I shouldn't get too close, mate," he said to Matthew, who was twenty metres away at square-leg. "I usually hit 'em pretty hard down there."

He took ages marking out his guard, then he looked up and said, "Right you are, bowler. I'm ready for you."

"Cocky, isn't he?" said Jacky to me. "Well, let's see what he makes of this."

He ran in and bowled a yorker which hit Hogg on the toe. Unfortunately, it was going down the leg side but Jacky made the most of the lbw appeal.

"Are you blind?" shouted Darren hopping about on one foot. "That was more like a wide."

Unfortunately Jacky didn't bowl very well after that. He started straying down the leg side again and feeding Darren Hogg's only shot, the swing to leg. I don't know whether Jacky was still trying to prove something to Clive, or maybe he was showing off in front of his brother – but once again he was trying to bowl much too fast and losing control.

I bowled at the other end. I had two good lbw shouts turned down in my first two overs and Cal missed a difficult, diving catch off spotty Hogg at square-leg. To be honest it was only really a half chance.

Cal came up to me at the end of the over. "Sorry, we needed that."

"How would you like to come on at Jacky's end after his next over?" I asked.

"Okay. But I'll need six fielders on the leg side to Hoggy."

Jacky's third over went for 10 runs and I don't think he was too disappointed to be taken off. Hoggy was having a lot of luck but he was scoring fast. We kept hearing his dad shouting, "Good shot, Darren," and "That's it, Darren, you show 'em." And Darren beamed and touched his cap in response.

I got rid of Phil Thacker in the next over with a quicker ball that nipped between bat and pad and splattered his wicket. A couple of balls later I got one to swing away from Hogg. There was a clear snick and Frankie went up with the ball in his hands appealing for the catch. So did I and everyone else in the team.

"Never touched it," said the Hogg with a scowl at me. And, unbelievably, the umpire didn't move.

Frankie was devastated. "What!" he said to Cal at slip. "My mum must have heard that at home."

The Hogg turned on him. "What are you, blind? My bat hit

the ground if you must know."

"And what made the ball change direction? The wind?"

"Be fair," said Cal. "He's saved me 50p."

"That's what I'm moaning about," said Frankie.

Old Sid who was umpiring at square-leg told them to get on with the game and I bowled again. This time it was a shorter ball which reared off the track. The Hogg went to swing it on the leg side but he was beaten for pace and the ball thumped into his ribs. He went down as if he'd been hit by a bus and writhed in agony on the ground. I rushed up to him thinking he was really hurt.

"You wait. I'll have you for that!" he snarled at me.

"Intimidatory bowling!" I heard the old Hogg shout as he jumped up from the scorers' bench and started running towards us.

"It was the pitch," I gasped. "The ball reared up." Bristly arrived panting at the wicket and pushed me aside roughly. "You want to watch it, sonny. Just wait till you're batting," he hissed in my ear and he bent over 'poor little Darren'.

Old Sid walked over and told Bristly that it wasn't my fault. And anyone could soon see that Darren wasn't the slightest bit hurt, though he kept rubbing his chest for ages and complaining about the pain. His old man slouched off mumbling to himself and, now and again, looking back at me with an unpleasant sneer.

Cal bowled his first over – a maiden. He got a couple of balls to turn a bit and then he bowled a beautiful floater which went straight on and beat the batsman all ends up.

In my last over I trapped the new batsman with a perfectly disguised slower ball. He went to swing it over mid-on and finished up spooning a catch to Erica at mid-wicket.

I nearly got another with my next ball. It just missed off-stump on the way through to Frankie. I finished my spell with brilliant figures: 4 overs; 1 maiden; 5 runs; 2 wickets. Not bad! But they were on 29 for two after eight overs and it wasn't going to be an easy pitch to bat on.

Cal holds the ball in the normal off-spinner's grip but his index finger lies alongside the seam and the thumb is behind the ball. As the ball is bowled, the first finger pushes the ball towards the slips instead of spinning it. It's called a 'floater' or sometimes an 'arm ball'.

Spotty Hogg swung Cal for 4 and 2 off the first two balls of his next over. Cal had six fielders on the leg side and, as usual, he was giving the ball a lot of air. I kept saying to myself, "Don't worry, he'll hole out sooner or later." But I was getting worried.

Cal bowled another loopy off-break and this one must have had a bit of extra bounce off the pitch. Hoggy went for his swing and the ball took a top edge and went high in the air. Cal called for it and stepped forward to take a simple catch. Spotty Hogg went tearing down the wicket and, as the ball landed in Cal's cupped hands, the Hogg ran straight into him, knocking him flying. Cal stood up, furious, but the ball was still safely in his hands.

"You . . ." Cal's got a terrible temper when he's roused and I thought for a moment he was going to hurl the ball at Darren. Then he controlled himself and turned to the umpire. "How is that?" he said very slowly and he held the ball out accusingly at Hogg.

"Hard luck, Darren," came the shout from the scorers' bench and Darren departed without a word of apology to Cal.

"That was deliberate," said Cal. "He tried to make it look like an accident but he ran straight at me."

"I know," I said. "I wonder how many more nasty tricks the Hoggs have got in store for us?"

The scoring rate dropped dramatically as the next two batsmen had to deal with some accurate bowling from Cal and Erica, who came on at my end. But we didn't take another wicket until the fifteenth over when Tylan had two in three balls. Both of them clean bowled. They were 54 for five.

Erica got an lbw in her last over and I brought on Clive at the bottom end. He took a wicket with his first ball – a good diving catch by Frankie.

Frankie grinned at Cal. "One to me, okay?"

"Can't argue with that," said Cal. "But I'll win it back soon, you'll see."

It was sooner than he thought. A top edge next over bounced into Frankie's gloves and bounced out again. Like all catches when the keeper's standing up, it was a difficult one. But it was still worth 50p to Cal.

It didn't matter much because the batsman was run out next ball by a sharp throw from Erica which hit the stumps and the last two wickets fell in two balls – a caught and bowled by Tylan and a yorker from Clive that took middle and off-stumps.

They were all out for 64. Tylan had taken three for 7 and Clive . . .

"Two for 2 off seven balls. New attack bowler discovered!" he bragged with a telling look at Jacky.

"Yeah – bowling at rabbits," sneered Jacky. "A class bat would murder a trundler like you."

"Just stand aside and give me the chance," said Clive. "And by the way, how many runs did you go for? Seven an over was it?"

HOME TEAM	GRUNTY DYKE	V	GLORY GARDENS	AWAY TEAM	AT GRUNTY DYKE DATE MAY 19th

INNINGS OF **GRUNTY DYKE** .... TOSS ~~CLAIMED~~ WON BY **G.D.** WEATHER **DRY**

BATSMAN	RUNS SCORED	HOW OUT	BOWLER	SCORE
1 D. HOGG	1.1.1.4.2.4.1.1.1.4.2 ››	c & b	SEBASTIEN	22
2 P. THACKER	2.1.1.1.2.2.1 ››	bowled	KNIGHT	10
3 N. MOBBS	1. ››	c† DAVIES	KNIGHT	1
4 G. QUERNPECKER	1.2.1.1.2.1 ››	RUN	OUT	8
5 A. KEMP	1.2.1 ››	bowled	VELLACOTT	4
6 B. BATTERSBEE	››	bowled	VELLACOTT	0
7 D. BUDDLE	1.2 ››	lbw	DAVIES	3
8 C. STOREY	1.2.1 ››	c† ALLEN	DA COSTA	4
9 P. ENNIS	2 ››	c & b	VELLACOTT	2
10 H. BATTERSBEE	1 ››	bowled	DA COSTA	1
11 F. HARD	-	NOT	OUT	0

FALL OF WICKETS											BYES	2.1			3	TOTAL EXTRAS	9
SCORE	27	29	35	53	53	56	61	63	64	64	L.BYES	1.1.1			3	TOTAL	64
											WIDES	1.1			2	FOR	
BAT NO	2	3	1	5	6	7	8	4	9	10	NO BALLS	1			1	WKTS	10

SCORE AT A GLANCE

BOWLING ANALYSIS · NO BALL + WIDE														OVS	MDS	RUNS	WKT
BOWLER	1	2	3	4	5	6	7	8	9	10	11	12	13				
1 J. GUNN	.1 2.1.1	1.4 2•.	2.2.1 4•.1	✗										3	0	23	0
2 H. KNIGHT	.1 ..1	M	.1W •.1. W...:	✗										4	1	5	2
3 C. SEBASTIEN	M	4.2W ...: 2.•1	•.1 •.•: ..•2	✗										4	1	12	1
4 E. DAVIES	.1 1.•1	.1 ..•2	.•2 W.1	✗										4	0	9	1
5 T. VELLACOTT	.1W W.1	..2 0.•1	..: 1.W	✗										3	0	7	3
6 C. DA COSTA	W.. 2.	W												1.1	0	2	2
7																	
8																	
9																	

Chapter Nine

"**W**ell batted boys, 68," said old Hogg as we all walked off. He didn't even bother to clap us in.

"It's not 68, it's only 64," said Jo.

"You must have missed some runs, young lady," insisted the Hogg and he was off to talk to his team.

"He's cheating and he doesn't even know how to score," said Jo. She was really cross. "Look at this, it's all wrong." She showed us the Grunty Dyke score-book that Bristly had been scrawling in with his horrible handwriting.

"He puts byes and leg-byes down as runs against the bowler and he writes 'W' for a 'wide' when it means a 'wicket'. Of course he's got Darren scoring 26 instead of 22 which it should be. It's not worth playing cricket against stupid people like that."

"Don't worry, Jo. You'll feel better when we've given them a good hiding," said Frankie.

"It'd be easier if there were a score-board," said Jo. "Then you could keep a running check on the score."

"But what do we do about the extra four runs he's added on?" asked Erica.

"I'll have a word with Kiddo," I said.

"Can't see the Hogg taking much notice," said Tylan. "Look at him, he struts around like the Fat Controller."

"We'll just have to get 69," said Cal. "I think we should forget the Hoggs and concentrate on scoring the runs. It's a lousy pitch, but we can do it."

"Oh, that reminds me," said Jo. "Has anyone seen 'Gatting'?"

"Yes, I saw him with Kiddo a couple of minutes ago," said Jason.

"I don't mean that Gatting," said Jo. "I mean our 'Gatting', the mascot. He's normally in the team bag, but I can't find him anywhere."

"Oh no," I said under my breath. My sister Lizzie had spent hours making that stupid mascot for us. She'd kill me if we'd lost it.

It's supposed to be a Gatting lookalike but I can't see it myself. It *is* black and rather fat like Gatting but apart from that . . . well, it doesn't even look like a dog; it's more like a little, black pig. Jo's very fond of it, though. She says it brings us luck. It hasn't done very well so far, mind you.

"Who saw it last?" I asked.

"We had him at the end of the Mudlarks game," said Erica.

"We could easily have left it behind with all the bother with Azzie and the ambulance," said Jason.

"I think I saw it in the bag at Nets on Saturday," said Cal.

"Well, he's not there now," said Jo.

I went off to find Kiddo who was walking the real Gatting round the ground. I think he was keeping out of old Hogg's way. I told him about the difference in the score-books and Jo's complaints.

"I think it would be best to assume you need 69 to win," he said. "We can't prove that Jo's got it right, can we? Though I have to admit, it's pretty likely she has."

"Have you ever seen her make a mistake?"

"No," said Kiddo. "Tell you what, kiddo, I'll keep an independent check on the score from over here while you're batting. Just make sure you get 69."

A few moments later Cal and Matthew walked out to open the Glory Gardens innings. It began with a controversial run out. Cal called for a quick single and the throw beat Matt to the bowler's end; but the bowler seemed to fumble the ball and knock the bails off with his hands.

"Not out," shouted Frankie. "He didn't have the ball in his hands, umpire."

"Outrageous," said Tylan.

But the bowler insisted he'd hit the wicket with the ball and their umpire gave Matt out. The bowler, in case you hadn't guessed, was spotty Hogg.

He bowled quite fast with an awkward slinging action. We could see he was deliberately pitching the ball short which made it difficult to judge the bounce on the hard, uneven surface.

Clive immediately got one that reared up at him and hit him on the shoulder.

"That's my boy, Darren," shouted Bristly Hogg. "Put some beef into it! Hit the deck!" If anything was intimidatory bowling this was – but that didn't seem to bother old Hoggy now we were on the receiving end.

Clive got another short, lifting ball but this time he stepped inside it and hooked it for four.

Spotty Hogg glared at him and walked back to his mark. He ran in again and unleashed a head-high beamer and Clive only ducked under it at the last moment. It beat the keeper and went for four byes.

Old Sid had had enough. He walked over to the Grunty umpire and, after a short conference, both umpires gave Hoggy an official warning. He protested that the ball had slipped, of course, but no one believed him except 'you know who'.

"Those umpires don't know the rules," Bristly protested loudly. "Time yours was pensioned off anyway." Good thing old Sid didn't hear him.

Thacker, the bowler at the other end, was almost as quick as Hoggy and he too got some wicked bounce out of the pitch. I was just thinking of how Marty would have been almost unplayable on this track, when Thacker got one to rise extra steeply and Clive just failed to get his glove out of the way. The keeper took the catch and the Grunties and old Hoggy on the scorers' bench all went up in a deafening appeal. Clive walked off without waiting for the decision.

"Rats!" said Frankie. "I wanted Clive to get 50 today. I could even stand his boasting if we beat this lot."

For once, Erica didn't stay for long. She got a rare, well-pitched-up delivery from Hogg and, trying too hard to take full advantage of it, she drove it in the air straight to extra cover. I was in.

"What's the score?" I asked Jo as I walked past her.

"22 for three," she said.

This is the wicket-keeper's view of Clive playing the hook shot. His head is outside the line of the ball and look at the position of his feet. He watches the ball on to his bat and hits it behind square-leg for four.

"21!" corrected the Hogg.

Jo looked at him in disbelief.

"Make up your minds," I said.

Cal met me on my way to the wicket. "Ready for some serious sledging?" he asked with a smile.

"What d'you mean?"

"A running commentary," he said. "And not all that nice at times. You'll see."

As I half expected, spotty Hogg greeted me with a bouncer which I ducked under and the umpire called a wide. Hoggy followed through and finished only a couple of yards away from me. "Next one gets your head," he snarled.

I stared back at him. So, that was the way he wanted to play it.

Cal scored two 2s off the next over, leaving me still to get off the mark and facing Hogg's final over. He was bowling flat out and I decided to leave as many balls as I could. He overstepped the line a couple of times, trying to bowl extra fast. The keeper and slip kept talking as he ran up to bowl which made it really hard to concentrate. I knew they were doing it on purpose.

At last I got a juicy half-volley just outside the off-stump and I leaned into it. The ball sped past extra-cover for 4. I gave Hoggy a huge grin. "I'll get you, mate," he hissed.

Three balls of the over to go. I was determined he wouldn't get my wicket. The angrier he gets the better, I thought. So when I heard the keeper muttering in the middle of Hoggy's run up, I stepped away from the crease. "Sorry, bowler, a fly," I said wafting away the imaginary insect. And Hoggy had to walk all the way back to his mark.

He bowled a wide and another – the second one beat the keeper and went for four. This way we'd win on wides and no balls. Now he was really frothing at the mouth. He tried the beamer again but only managed a low full toss which I should have hit for four but I decided to play safe and block it. The last ball of the over was down the leg side and I glanced it neatly for a single. 12 runs had come off the over. We'd steamed along to 39 for three.

The two new bowlers were almost as quick as the opening pair. They both tried to bowl too fast and there were plenty of loose balls to score off. But on this pitch you never felt 'in'. And it seemed to be getting worse as the game went on with balls popping up off a length or shooting along the ground.

It was a shooter that did for Cal in the tenth over. Then Jason got a horrible delivery before he was seeing the ball properly. He fended it off and the ball lobbed into the hands of spotty Hogg at slip. He made it look like a brilliant catch by diving after he had caught it and he followed it up by doing a lap of honour, holding the ball in the air and cheering.

"Great catch, Darren," shouted Bristly, beaming all over his stupid face.

Tylan told me the score when he came in. We had reached 55 for five and there were nine overs to go.

Tylan and I put on another nine precious runs although both of us were dropped; Tylan at mid-off and me in the slips by Hoggy.

I gave him a sarcastic look and said, "Oh, hard luck, skipper," and, for once, he couldn't think of anything to say but he looked extremely sick.

Tylan went to a good catch from the bowler and Frankie decided as usual that he'd win the game with a six and missed a straight ball which knocked out his middle stump.

"Sorry, Hooker," he said. "Still, only five to win. We'll do it."

It was down to me and the Gunn brothers, because you could forget Ohbert. Brian Gunn turned out to be just as much a slogger as Jacky had said. He swung one ball away for two and hit the next straight up in the air. The keeper took the catch and in came Jacky. He immediately played a nervous stab at a straight one and was clean bowled. We'd slumped to 67 for nine. And Ohbert was in!

Fortunately, Jacky had been bowled by the last ball of the

over, so I was facing. I tried to clear my mind and concentrate. I mustn't give the bowling to Ohbert. I told him not to run unless I shouted. I also remembered that Hoggy's score-book had been one run short when I came in to bat. Best be on the safe side and aim for 70, I thought. But the main thing was not to get out.

I was nearly bowled first ball. I got my bat down on a shooter just in time. The next I pushed backward of square-leg but there was only a single in it. I nearly shouted "No" to Ohbert. Then I thought if I shout anything he'll run so I just stared at him and shook my head.

"Could have run two there," mocked the wicket-keeper.

At last I got a short ball and I hooked. I felt it connect with the middle of the bat and I screamed at Ohbert, "RUN!"

And to give Ohbert his due he ran – flat out, with his extra large tee-shirt billowing out behind him. I could see the ball was being held up in the long grass and wouldn't quite go for four. But there were easily three runs in it. "That's it, Ohbert," I said, as we crossed for the third. "Keep going."

I arrived at the bowler's crease and looked up. We'd done it. 70 runs. I raised my bat in triumph and suddenly saw that Ohbert was still running, back towards me.

"No, Ohbert. Stop!" I shouted. But he kept coming. I thought quickly. If I ran and we crossed before the run out, then the third run would count. I sprinted towards the keeper's end, knowing the throw was coming in. As I passed Ohbert, I shouted, "You daft idiot." The throw was a good one, right over the stumps and I was run out by a yard. But we'd crossed, we'd won, we'd still got 70 runs.

Up went the cheers from the Glory Gardens team.

"Well batted, Hooker," shouted Cal.

"You can stop running now, Ohbert," yelled Frankie.

And then we heard the voice of the Hogg. "Wait a minute," he said. "You've only got 67, so Grunty Dyke are the winners."

There was pandemonium. The Grunties led by spotty Darren started to jump about and jeer at us.

"That's nonsense," said Jo, almost in tears. "We won. We won by six whole runs."

"I'm afraid you just don't know how to score properly, my girl," said Bristly Hogg. "I think you'll find this is the official score-book."

Kiddo arrived on the scene. He took one look at old Hogg and said, "I shall be reporting this to the Colts Association." He told us all to get our gear together and get in the minibus. We left without saying another word. Old Sid followed us in his car looking very unhappy about the way things had turned out.

Kiddo didn't speak until we were out of the ground.

"I want you to know that as far as I'm concerned, kiddoes, you won. I shall ask both umpires to send in a match report and the score-books will be sent to the Association. I kept the score throughout your innings and Jo got it completely right."

"Course she did. She's perfect," said Frankie.

Jo kicked him.

"And what if the Association believe Hoggy instead of us?" asked Cal.

"We lose," said Kiddo. "But let's wait and see. Till then, you'd best try and forget about it. You've got another game next week to think about. Let's hope it's a proper game of cricket."

HOME TEAM	GRUNTY DYKE	V	GLORY GARDENS	AWAY TEAM	AT GRUNTY DYKE DATE MAY 19TH

INNINGS OF GLORY GARDENS   TOSS WON BY G.D.?   WEATHER DRY

BATSMAN	RUNS SCORED	HOW OUT	BOWLER	SCORE
1 M. ROSE		RUN	OUT	0
2 C. SEBASTIEN	2.1.1.1.2.2.1	lbw	MOBBS	10
3 C. DACOSTA	4.2.1.	ct BATTERSBEE B	THACKER	7
4 E. DAVIES	2	ct STOREY	HOGG	2
5 H. KNIGHT	4.1.2.2.1.1.2.1.2.1.3	RUN	OUT	23
6 J. PADGETT		ct HOGG	BUDDLE	0
7 T. VELLACOTT	1.1.	c x b	MOBBS	2
8 F. ALLEN		bowled	BUDDLE	0
9 B. GUNN	2.	ct BATTERSBEE B	BUDDLE	2
10 J. GUNN		bowled	BUDDLE	0
11 P. BENNETT		NOT	OUT	0

FALL OF WICKETS

	1	2	3	4	5	6	7	8	9	10
SCORE	0	18	22	51	55	64	65	67	67	70
BAT NO	1	3	4	2	6	7	8	9	10	5

BYES	4.1	5	TOTAL EXTRAS 24
L.BYES	1.1.	2	TOTAL 70
WIDES	1.1.4.1.1.1.1.1.	13	FOR
NO BALLS	1.1.1.	4	WKTS 10

SCORE AT A GLANCE

BOWLING ANALYSIS ⊙ NO BALL + WIDE																	
BOWLER	1	2	3	4	5	6	7	8	9	10	11	12	13	OVS	MDS	RUNS	WKT
1 D. HOGG	..⊙..|.1.2 ⊙.⊙. / 4.. .2.| +W. + +													4	0	26	1
2 P. THACKER	..|. ⊙.W. .2.| ..2 .2. .2. +..													4	0	12	1
3 D. BUDDLE	.|. 2.1 ++.| 1W. 2.| +W. .2 2WW													4	0	15	4
4 N. MOBBS	+... ..2 ..+. ... 1.W. .1 W.. 3													3.4	0	10	2
5																	
6																	
7																	
8																	
9																	

Chapter Ten

"It's not fair," said Jason.

"Outrageous!" muttered Tylan.

It was Saturday morning and we were all staring at the notice board in the Priory pavilion. Thursday evening's result confirmed what we all knew; we were bottom of the League.

Grunty Dyke *beat* Glory Gardens by one run
Wyckham Wanderers *lost to* Old Courtiers by 12 runs
Mudlarks *beat* Barmewell by five wickets

	Played	W	L	Points
Old Courtiers	3	3	0	30
Wyckham Wanderers	3	2	1	20
Mudlarks	3	1	1	12*
Barmewell	3	1	2	10
Grunty Dyke	3	1	2	10
Glory Gardens	3	0	2	2*

*The game between Mudlarks and Glory Gardens ended in no result

"How long will it take for Kiddo's appeal to go through?" asked Erica.

"At least two or three weeks," I said.

"Until then we're bottom of the League," said Marty.

"We won't be if we win the next two games," said Jo.

"Oh yeah! Some hope – against Wyckham and Old Courtiers," said Marty. "They're only first and second, aren't they? We can't even beat the worst teams in the League."

Marty was even gloomier than usual.

"We *did* beat Grunty Dyke," insisted Jo.

"And we'll win the appeal," said Erica.

"Hoggs might fly!" said Tylan.

"That was a good win for Old Courtiers against Wyckham," said Matthew, changing the subject.

"Kiddo always said Old Courtiers were the best team in the League," I said.

"Where do you think they got their name from?" said Frankie. "I bet they're dead posh and say things like 'How is that, sire?' and 'Would you pray care to take a single?'"

We ignored him. I asked Marty if he'd be fit for Thursday's game.

"Probably, worse luck," he said glumly. He didn't mean it, of course – because he's mad about cricket. Everyone knows Marty's a terrible pessimist but I'd never seen him quite so fed up. He didn't bowl at Nets because his ankle was still a bit swollen but he did have a bat.

Azzie's still out of the team though. He's having a check up at the hospital next week and if it's okay he'll probably play in the last League game after half term. He wasn't at Nets, nor was Cal – it was his turn on the Knicker Rota. Everyone else turned up. Even Clive arrived on time. Brian Gunn came, too. His batting turned out to be just as bad as it had looked in the Grunty game. He's a swing-and-hope sort of batsman and he usually misses. But he did connect with one ball from Tylan which went straight over the hedge at the end of the ground. It was a huge hit and we couldn't find the ball.

Brian's a bit bossy for my liking. Maybe it's because he's older than all of us and he feels he has to behave big. He'd quickly joined his brother, Matthew and Jason in the 'anti-Clive' gang and it wasn't long before he took over as leader.

I noticed him trying to wind Clive up several times. The worst occasion was when Clive was batting. I bowled him with a perfect in-cutter; it was a beaut and Clive looked up and nodded at me as if to say 'Well bowled'. Then Brian jumped in, "Got him, Hooker! Did you see *that*, everyone? Mr Clever loses his furniture."

"Since when have you known anything about batting or bowling?" said Clive with a sneer.

"I know a fat head when I see it," said Brian looking round for support from Jason and Jacky. I told Brian and Clive to shut up but, to be honest, I was thinking more about what a brilliant ball I'd bowled. I'd been practising it for weeks.

Kiddo came over to see what the trouble was but Jo changed the subject.

"Francis definitely needs some wicket-keeping practice," she said to Kiddo.

"I thought he did quite well in the last match," said Kiddo with a smile.

"Apart from the dropped catch and five byes," said Jo.

"No one's perfect," said Frankie. "Except my sister."

Kiddo showed him how to stand up to the stumps for the slower bowlers. He got Tylan to bowl at the wicket with Frankie crouched behind it.

"The main thing is concentration," he said. We all know Frankie's a bit short on that.

We were half way through Nets when a stocky, fair-haired boy who I'd never seen before walked over to us. He had amazing freckles and a big, wide smile.

"Hiya, Clive," he said as he got close.

Clive looked up and said hello. He began to introduce the boy to me.

"Hooker, this is . . . eh . . ."

"Tracy McCurdy," said the boy in a strange accent. He shook hands. "But I guess you can call me 'Mack' if you'd rather, 'cos everyone seems to think Tracy's a girl's name."

He told me he had just started going to Clive's school. His family had moved here from Australia. "Might be here for a couple of years, so I thought I'd better make the most of it and find a good cricket team. Clive here tells me that Glory Gardens is pretty fair. Mind if I join in your practice?"

Frankie comes up with the bounce of the ball and moves into position, getting behind the line. Look at the position of his hands. He is likely to hurt his fingers taking a catch like this! His fingers should be angled more so that they are not facing the ball directly.

I liked Mack from the start. Everyone did. Mind you, we all called him Mack and not Tracy. I couldn't help wondering how he'd got a name like that, but maybe there are lots of boys called Tracy in Australia. Funny thing, though – no one, not even Frankie, ever mentioned his real name again.

I watched him in the nets with great interest. His bowling wasn't bad – about as good as Clive's. He was a reasonable bat, too – another left-hander like Clive, which was good news. But he couldn't have been more different from Clive in every other way. He simply buzzed with enthusiasm. And he never stopped talking.

"Jeez, great ball, mate!" he said when I knocked out his off-stump with a corker. "You'd better show me how you do that."

Mack had definitely been taught his cricket well. But it was his fielding which really amazed me. He buzzed about, ran for everything and he had the best pick up and throw I'd ever seen. What's more he could throw just as well with either hand.

After Nets we chose the team for the game on Thursday. With Marty back, the Selection Committee had to decide who to drop. We could only play one from Ohbert, Brian and Mack. Marty and I voted for Mack – after all it was the Wyckham game and we needed a win badly. But Jo thought Ohbert should be in the team.

"He's been with Glory Gardens right from the start and he's never let us down," she said.

"What about running me out in the last game," I said.

"Look, this Mack's only just turned up and we don't know anything about him," said Jo. "I know Ohbert's pretty hopeless, but I happen to think he's part of Glory Gardens."

"Perhaps he should be the replacement mascot," said Marty unkindly.

I didn't want to be reminded of that. I still hadn't told Lizzy about it.

In the end Marty and I outvoted Jo and this was the team we picked.

Matthew Rose	Mack McCurdy
Cal Sebastien	Tylan Vellacott
Clive da Costa	Frankie Allen
Erica Davies	Jacky Gunn
Hooker Knight	Marty Lear
Jason Padgett	

Ohbert took it pretty well. But none of us had expected the row caused by Brian. Clive started it. He was standing next to

Brian looking at the team sheet on the notice board. "Beginning to look like a proper team," he said. "Now we've got rid of the rubbish."

"I don't want to play in a team with a half-wit like you," said Brian.

"Just as well 'cause you're not."

"Don't push it, Clive. You might end up on the injured list," said Brian.

"Dream on," said Clive, turning and walking away. Brian stuck out a foot and caught him off balance and Clive fell sharply and banged his head against a chair. He wasn't hurt but Jacky made the mistake of laughing at him as he got up. Clive took a swing at him and his fist caught Jacky on the chest and sent him flying. Jacky's glasses shot across the pavilion floor and disappeared under a table. Next thing Brian was charging head down at Clive. They both collapsed in a tangled heap on the floor punching and clawing at each other.

Fortunately Kiddo saw it all and he quickly pulled them apart before anyone got hurt.

"Right, I've had enough. One more stupid row like this and you're both out of the team," he said. He looked at us one by one. "And that applies to anyone who'd rather fight than play cricket. Understood?"

"I'm leaving anyway," said Brian and he walked out followed by Jacky.

Clive slumped into a chair and didn't say a word. He just stared straight ahead without looking at anyone.

"I don't know what's the matter with you lot, especially you, Clive," said Kiddo. "Just when I think you're turning into a half-reasonable cricket team, I find you at each other's throats. Cricket's not just about playing and winning, you know. It's about being fair and decent."

"What about Grunty Dyke, then?" asked Tylan. "I don't call them fair and decent."

"You might be right," said Kiddo. "But when you play cricket, you rely on people being straight – and most of them are. I hope you are all the sort of cricketers who will walk when you know you're out and won't complain when a decision goes against you. Because if you don't play that way you might just as well not bother. What's the pleasure in winning if you have to cheat to do it?"

"Well, old Hoggy seemed pretty happy," said Frankie.

"He reminds me of someone I used to play against in County Cricket," said Kiddo.

"Oh no! What have I done?" whispered Frankie to me. "I've only set him off on one of his stories."

There was no stopping Kiddo now. "I remember, he was captain of a County side," he said. "I won't tell you which one. And he told everyone in the team that if they ever walked for a caught behind or a bat-pad catch he'd kick them out. He was like Mr Hogg, you see – he wanted to win so much that he didn't care how.

One day a new player joined the team and, in spite of the captain's warning, he walked for a catch behind the wicket even though the umpire hadn't heard the snick. The captain went wild and told him he'd never play again. But the rest of the team had had enough. They were too professional to go on strike or to refuse to play properly but they started playing fair. They walked for catches, and once even for an lbw. They called opposition batsmen back when they didn't think they were out. On one occasion, the captain took a 'catch' which bounced in front of him. "How's that!" he appealed. "Not out," shouted the wicket-keeper. Another time, a fielder signalled four runs because even though he'd stopped the ball crossing the boundary, his foot had been over the line at the moment of contact.

The captain went crazy every time this happened. One by one he dropped his best players and brought in second team players whom he thought he could bully. And, of course, the team started to lose.

To cut a long story short . . ."

("Let it be true," whispered Frankie.)

" . . . the team slumped to the bottom of the League and the captain was sacked. Next season, under a new captain, they won the County Championship outright." He looked around at his audience.

"And that's the way I want you lot to play. Okay, kiddoes?"

We all nodded, apart from Clive who sat there still staring into space.

"You'd better get off home for lunch, then," said Kiddo and he walked over to talk to Clive on his own.

As we left Mack came up to me. "Jeez," he said. "If it's as exciting as this at your practice sessions, what are the games like?"

———————————— ● ————————————

I had a lot to tell Cal that afternoon. I gave him the full story about Mack and Clive and Brian and Jacky and Kiddo's lecture.

"Sounds like I chose a good Saturday to work for Tylan's old man," he said.

"What do you think I should do about the team for Thursday?"

"Well, if Azzie were fit I'd drop them all – Clive, Brian and Jacky," he said. "It may not have been all down to Clive this time but he's always winding people up."

"I think I'm going to ring Jacky and tell him I still want him to play," I said.

"And if he won't?"

"Then we'll pick Ohbert."

"It's a stroke of luck this Aussie turning up," said Cal. "You say he's a friend of Clive?"

"They're at school together," I said.

We went into the kitchen to phone Jacky and there was Lizzie looking furious.

"I've got something to say to you, Harry Knight," she said. She only calls me Harry when she's angry. Oh no, I thought, she must have heard about 'Gatting'.

"We've only mislaid it," I said. "We'll find it, I promise."

"Find what?" said Lizzie. A nasty feeling came over me. "What are you talking about?" she said.

Oh no! She didn't know about 'Gatting'. But it was too late now. I know my sister, once she thinks something's being kept from her, she goes on and on until you tell her. She never gives up. So I went for the only way out. The truth. "We've lost 'Gatting', your eh . . . our mascot."

"I don't believe it! How?"

"It'll turn up. I mean who would want to steal it?" said Cal trying to help but making things ten times worse.

"I see," said Lizzy. "Well, that's the last thing I ever do for you and your rotten cricket team." And she stormed out of the kitchen slamming the door.

"Thanks, Cal," I said. "You were a great help."

"At least she forgot what she was going to say to you," said Cal.

"Let's say you don't know my sister," I said. "She's got a memory like an elephant."

I rang Jacky and Brian answered the phone. I could tell he was still angry. "What do you want?" he said.

I started to say I wanted to speak to Jacky but he broke in, "Is Clive still in your team?"

"Er . . . yes, I think so," I said feebly.

"Then I'm not. And nor's Jacky." And he put the phone down on me.

"Sounds like, come back Ohbert all is forgiven," said Cal.

Chapter Eleven

"Having a really good season, aren't you?" said Liam Katz sarcastically as we went out to toss. "What is it – two points so far?"

"We beat the Grunties last week, only they cheated," I said.

"You surprise me," said Liam. "They ought to be kicked out of the League if you ask me."

"Anyway, you lost last week, didn't you?" I asked. You have to keep reminding Liam that he's not quite as good as he thinks he is – i.e. perfect. He's a great cricketer but he's even better at telling you how good he is.

"We should have won easily," he said, "but the batting collapsed when I got out. I got 41 and I was really choked. If we'd beaten them we'd have won the League. Now I can't see anyone stopping Old Courtiers."

He won the toss and chose to bat.

"Oh just one thing," I said as we were walking off. "Have you still got that umpire you had last year?" When we last played Wyckham their umpire had been almost as biased as old Hoggy.

Liam smiled, "You mean Whitey. No, he's given up umpiring. I think he was getting a bit short-sighted."

That was one way of putting it. Still I was relieved to hear it. So was everyone else when I told them.

The Glory Gardens team was as selected on Saturday except Ohbert was in for Jacky. Ohbert was pleased (as far as you can tell with Ohbert). I hadn't heard a thing from Jacky or Brian Gunn. I knew we'd miss Jacky badly; he's a good bowler, although he's been a bit below par lately, and he's a real team player, too.

The game started bang on five o'clock.

Liam came out to bat with a tall left-hander called Luke. There were a lot of new, older players in the Wyckham side and he was one of them. Apart from Liam, I knew only Win Reifer and Charlie Gale. It just shows what a good cricketer Liam is. He's captain even though he's just about the youngest in the team.

Marty's first over was a bit off target. His run up wasn't quite right; maybe he was still nervous about his ankle. Liam's the worst person to bowl at when your direction is off. He helped himself to two 4s.

But you can never write Marty off and the next over he dropped his pace and bowled a lot straighter. He was really unlucky not to get Liam with a snick outside off-stump. It just failed to carry to Frankie.

Meanwhile I was bowling at the other end – and bowling pretty well. I had two lbw appeals turned down; one against each batsman. Then Liam pushed a ball to the left of cover-point and called for a single. The batsman at the other end was backing up and ran immediately but Mack swooped on the ball, picked up and threw left-handed. He had one stump to aim at and his throw hit it half way down. A direct hit! The batsman was run out by at least a metre.

"Wow! Where did he come from?" gasped Liam in amazement.

I smiled. They'd think twice about taking quick singles from now on, I thought.

The game was held up for a bit because Frankie had seriously split his trousers running up to the stumps and, although he wanted to carry on, Cal told him that he'd get arrested.

"Anyway I can't concentrate on fielding with the sight of your red underpants every time you bend down," said Cal.

While he was changing I had a word with Cal and Marty about how to get Liam out.

"He likes to hook and cut," said Cal. "So maybe we should set a trap for him."

"Such as?" said Marty.

"Well, two gullies and a deep backward square-leg and then drop a few short at him."

"If it doesn't work it'll cost a lot of runs," I said.

"Why not give it a try next over," said Marty. "I've only got one left anyhow."

I bowled my third over and the new batsman hit me for four over mid-wicket but I immediately bowled him next ball with a peach of a yorker.

At the end of the over I set the field Marty wanted. I went into the gully with Cal standing a few feet to my left and I put Erica out at backward square-leg on the boundary because she's one of the best catchers in the team. Marty's first two balls were wide outside the off-stump and Liam crashed them both into the gully area. The first was stopped by Cal diving to his left; the second went between us all along the ground for four. Then Marty bowled a fast lifting ball on leg stump and Liam went for the hook. He got a top edge and the ball flew high off the bat. For a second it looked as if Erica hadn't picked it up. She stood still judging the length of the catch and then she ran in at full pace. Would she make it? We all watched as the ball fell faster and faster and . . . Erica swooped in and took it on the run at knee height.

"It worked!" shouted Marty.

"Beaut catch," yelled Mack.

Liam sloped off looking sick and realising he'd fallen straight into our trap.

"I'm glad to see the back of him," said Cal to me.

"Yeah, great plan of yours," I said.

"Just luck it worked," said Cal. "If he'd middled that shot it would have been a six and you'd all be cursing me."

Marty was bowling with a lot more spring in his step and

he beat the new batsman for pace with the second ball he bowled at him and over went the middle stump.

They'd slumped to 25 for four – *and* we'd got rid of Liam Katz.

Charlie Gale, their keeper, was now at the wicket. Charlie never stops talking – especially when he's batting. And Frankie's just as bad. It was hard to get them to shut up and play cricket.

"Don't think I'm going to fall for that hook trap," he said to Frankie. "You'll be wasting your time putting a fielder down there for me."

"Won't need to," said Frankie. "You can't hit it that far."

"Oh yeah?" said Charlie. "Then you watch carefully."

The batsman at the other end was called Yousef Mohamed. "He's our secret weapon," said Charlie. "Turns the ball a mile."

"Some secret," said Frankie.

So this was the brilliant spinner everyone had talked about. He and Charlie batted well together for several overs although the run rate fell. At the end of Marty's and my spells I brought on Erica and Clive and they both kept a tight line. With six overs to go, Wyckham were on 41 and I decided to rest Erica and see what Cal could do.

Charlie Gale was tempted straightaway by the slower bowling and he miscued to mid-wicket where Jason took the catch. Win Reifer arrived at the wicket and we all knew what he'd do. He missed the first two balls he received from Cal – but he was soon laying into the bowling and, for a time, I began to think we were going to throw away our grip on the game. To make things worse, Win's a left-handed bat and I started to get in a muddle with the fielders changing over every time for the left and right-handers.

A big four smacked back straight over Clive's head brought up the fifty.

Tylan came to the rescue as he often does against the sloggers. He deceived Win with a lovely floating delivery which turned and took a thick edge as he went for the big one over the bowler's head. The ball flew straight to me at wide mid-on and I caught it chest high.

Two more wickets fell in quick succession, both to Tylan, as the Wyckham players tried to push along the scoring rate. As Cal began the last over they were 60 for eight. Yousef the spinner twice pulled him for two runs – then Cal clean bowled the new batsman with a ball which turned sharply from outside off-stump. It surprised me to see so much turn and I'm sure I saw Yousef smiling from the other end. You could see he was looking forward to having a bowl on this track.

With two balls to go Cal was driven hard through extra-cover and Clive and Mack went after it. Clive's quick but Mack beat him to the ball easily. He picked up ten metres in from the boundary, turned and threw. The batsmen were well into the second run as he unleashed his throw. The ball hummed through the air low and fast, and it smacked into Frankie's gloves inches over the bails. He hardly had to move to break the wicket.

"Out!" said the umpire.

"Rageous!" said Tylan.

"Brilliant!" yelled Frankie to Mack. "Best throw I've ever seen."

Wyckham were all out for 66 with a ball to spare. We'd scored more than that in every game so far but I didn't need reminding that it would be tough to get the runs – especially against the demon spinner.

"Good team effort, kiddo," said Kiddo to me as we came off. "Now all you have to do is concentrate. Plenty of time. Just settle down and pick them off."

HOME TEAM	GLORY GARDENS V WYCKHAM WNDRS	AWAY TEAM	AT EASTGATE P. DATE MAY 26TH

INNINGS OF WYCKHAM WANDERERS	TOSS WON BY W.W. WEATHER BRIGHT

BATSMAN	RUNS SCORED	HOW OUT	BOWLER	SCORE
1 L. KATZ	4·4·1·2·1·4	ct DAVIES	LEAR	16
2 L. GONSALVES	1·	RUN	OUT	1
3 K. BASTIN	2·4	bowled	KNIGHT	6
4 G. RUMBELLOW		bowled	LEAR	0
5 C. GALE	1·1·1·2·1·3·1	ct PADGETT	SEBASTIEN	10
6 Y. MOHAMED	1·1·1·1·2·1·2·2·1	NOT	OUT	13
7 N. REIFER	2·2·4·1·2	ct KNIGHT	VELLACOTT	11
8 G. BURGESS	1·1	c x b	VELLACOTT	2
9 A. SAMI	1·	bowled	VELLACOTT	1
10 N. CARTER		bowled	SEBASTIEN	0
11 T. WOOD	1·	RUN	OUT	1

FALL OF WICKETS											BYES		TOTAL EXTRAS	5
SCORE	11	21	25	25	41	53	58	60	65	66	L BYES 1·1·1	3	TOTAL	66
BAT NO	2	3	1	4	5	7	8	9	10	11	WIDES 1·1	2	FOR	10
											NO BALLS		WKTS	

SCORE AT A GLANCE

BOWLING ANALYSIS ⊙ NO BALL + WIDE																	
BOWLER	1	2	3	4	5	6	7	8	9	10	11	12	13	OVS	MDS	RUNS	WKT
1 M. LEAR	·4·4 ·4·	··1 ··	·2· 1··	·4W ·W·	✗									4	0	17	2
2 H. KNIGHT	··1 ··	··1 ··	·· ···	·4W M										4	1	7	1
3 E. DAVIES	··1 ··	2·· ·1·	·3	✗										3	0	8	0
4 C. DA COSTA	1·· ·1·	·· 11·	·· 1·4	·1 4·1	✗									4	0	12	0
5 C. SEBASTIEN	·W· ·22	✗	·+·1 ·2·	221 W1										2·5	0	14	2
6 T. VELLACOTT	·2· W·1	W·1 1·W												2	0	5	3
7																	
8																	
9																	

Chapter Twelve

We had three visitors in the changing room between innings – one welcome and two definitely not.

First of all Azzie put his head round the door.

"Frankie, I don't believe it," he said. "Not a single bye!"

"And, you may have noticed, I didn't use my head once," said Frankie.

"So what's new?" asked Cal.

It was great to see Azzie looking his old self again. He told us he was 'dead certain' to be available for the last game. That was in a fortnight because it was half term next week.

"Doesn't look as if you'll need me today," said Azzie.

"Shouldn't bet on it," said Cal. "They're a strong bowling side."

"Perhaps we can disguise you as Ohbert and send you in to bat," said Frankie.

"Wouldn't work," said Tylan. "To be convincing he'd have to get out first ball."

We grinned at Ohbert and he grinned back. He hadn't heard a thing because his Walkman was turned up so loud the beat was echoing round the changing room.

"You'll go deaf, Ohbert," said Mack.

Ohbert smiled again and nodded.

That was when my sister appeared in the doorway with her boring friend, Mavis Alberts. My heart sank.

"What are you doing here?" I asked. But I knew exactly why she'd come.

"I hope you know you'll never win another game," she said. "You'll be cursed with bad luck forever."

"No wonder you're bottom," said Mave the Grave, that's what Cal calls her because she's so miserable and serious.

"They're talking about the mascot, you know, 'Gatting'," explained Cal to a puzzled-looking Frankie.

"What that black, squidgy thing," said Frankie. He looked at Lizzy. "We've lost it."

"I'm aware of that," said Lizzy with a scowl. "But did you know it's bad luck to lose your team mascot? And did you know you'll never win another game until you find it?"

"Rubbish!" said Frankie. "We're going to win this one."

"You wait and see," said Lizzy with a mysterious smile and she walked off arm-in-arm with Mave who, as far as I can remember, has never smiled in her life.

"I think your sister's turning into a witch, Hooker, just like mine," said Frankie. "It must be an epidemic."

I wished I'd never seen the rotten mascot. But it was time to start our innings and I soon forgot all about it.

Liam Katz set an attacking field for his bowlers. He opened with Win Reifer one end and Luke Gonsalves at the other. There wasn't much to choose between them; they were both extremely quick. But if anything Luke was even faster than Win – that made him very fast.

Both Matthew and Cal were in trouble against them and Matt was lucky to survive a big lbw appeal. Cal got a nasty one on the elbow and, soon after, he was clean bowled off a no ball.

They stuck it out for five overs but, finally, Cal edged to the keeper and we were 15 for one. That was the only wicket to fall to the opening quickies. Matthew and Clive kept them out and by the end of their spell we had 23 on the board.

"Slow but steady, kiddoes," said Kiddo, "that's the way."

Frankie let out a long, slow yawn.

At last, Liam brought on the famous spinner from the top end.

"He's a leggie," said Tylan, "you can tell from the run up."

"He's a good leggie," said Frankie, as his first ball had Clive groping at thin air outside the off-stump. Clive played and missed twice more and finally stepped back to hit a ball on the off-side and was clean bowled.

"Oh no," said Marty, "if Clive can't play him no-one can."

"You wait," said Frankie. "I'll knock him over the top."

"If we have to rely on that, we've lost," said Cal.

Erica decided to use her pads to keep out the spinner – he was turning the ball a long way. Meanwhile Liam Katz came on at the other end bowling tight, accurate, medium-pace and the run rate slowed almost to a standstill. After twelve overs we'd scored only 27. That meant we now needed five an over.

Erica was finally caught off the spinner going for a forcing shot on the leg side and lifting the ball to square-leg.

"Outrageous!" said Tylan. "That was the googly. Did you see, it went the other way."

I wasn't too pleased to hear that because I was about to get a front-seat view of the famous spin bowler. I walked to the wicket slowly, trying to concentrate. "Get a good look at him first and try and get to the pitch of the ball," I reminded myself.

I took a leg stump guard and watched carefully as the first ball pitched outside my pads and turned. I went to play a leg glance and missed but the ball ran off my pads for a leg-bye. I was very relieved to get down the other end.

Matthew was playing the spinner better than anyone. He was using his feet well. I watched him step out of his crease and push one on the on-side for a couple of runs, but two balls later he was beaten in the flight by a ball which went straight on and he was stumped. That made it 30 for four.

It was 30 for five after Jason played inside a perfect leg-break which clipped his off-bail. I was beginning to believe in my sister's curse. It's funny what daft thoughts you have when you're batting.

Mack greeted me in the middle of the pitch with a slap on

Matthew isn't afraid to use his feet to the spinner. He takes three quick steps out of his crease to get to the pitch of the ball. But he must make sure he hits the ball.

the back and said, "That spinner, he's only got one over left, skip. Why don't we see him off and then give the rest some leather."

It was good advice. There was no point in trying to slog against Mohamed. He was turning the ball too much and bowling too accurately. Liam took himself off, with two of his overs still to go, and brought on his fifth bowler. This could be our chance, I thought.

The first ball was medium-pace outside the off-stump. I watched it go by. There was no movement off the pitch. The next was on the same line but slightly shorter and I stepped back and cracked it for four through cover-point.

A big cheer went up from the Glory Gardens bench and it was only then that I realised that it was my first scoring stroke. I pulled another short one for two and leg glanced a single to take the strike against the spinner. He was on a hat trick.

"Now," I kept saying to myself, "don't throw it away."

The field closed in. He tempted me with a tossed-up, flighted delivery. I smothered it with a forward defensive. He bowled a quicker one which turned sharply away from me. I got my bat out of the way just in time. He bowled a googly outside the off-stump. It turned into me and I jammed my bat down on it. Then he over-pitched on the leg stump and I forced him away for three past square-leg.

Mack left his first ball and it nearly bowled him round his legs. He swept the last ball of the over against the spin and it went for two. And that was the end of the famous leg spinner. He'd taken four for eight.

"Thought you were going to play him defensively," I said to Mack.

"Changed my mind when I realised I hadn't got a clue where the ball was going," he said. He looked up at the score-board. "Right, no problem now," he said. "25 to win; five overs to do it."

Mack was an even better batsman than he'd looked in the nets. Out in the middle his aggression paid off. He attacked the bowlers and, above all, the fielders. He nearly ran me out with one call for a short single but we both knew we had to take a few chances if we were going to win.

Liam came on again at the spinner's end and Mack smacked him for four with a flat bat straight over his head. Then he got a lucky edge over the keeper's head for a single.

Two overs left and we needed 10. Mack holed out at mid-wicket and left with a shrug and a thumbs up sign. Tylan missed the next three balls and got a single off the last ball of the over. So he was still on strike and we needed eight off six balls.

"If you hit it, run," I said to him.

"What if I miss?"

"Run," I said.

Tylan jammed his bat down on a yorker and ran. I beat the throw – a direct hit on the stumps – by inches.

The next ball was short and I cracked it wide of mid-on for two. Then I edged one for a single and Tylan managed another run off the next ball. We needed three off two balls. I looked around the field and wondered whether to back off and hit it on the on-side or go for the leg side swing. I decided on the swing.

The ball was perfect for me. Just short of a length and on middle stump. If I missed I was out but I didn't. I felt the ball hit the meat of the bat and it soared over mid-wicket. And over the boundary. I couldn't believe it. My first six!

And we'd won!

Tylan and I walked off to the applause of both teams.

"Well batted," said Liam. "I thought we had you on the run for a moment."

"Brilliant knock," said Cal patting me on the back.

"26 not out," said Jo.

I looked at her and then looked again. There in front of her on the table was 'Gatting'.

"Where did you find it!" I said to Jo in amazement.

"Oh, Kiddo gave it to me just after you went in to bat," said Jo. "You'll never believe who had it."

"Who?"

"Gatting. Kiddo found it in Gatting's kennel. We think he must have taken it out of our kit bag and smuggled it home."

"I think if Gatting likes it he should keep it," said Frankie.

"Oh no, he can't," said Jo. "It's our mascot. Look how we won as soon as we got it back."

"Don't be stupid. That was just a coincidence," said Frankie.

"Maybe," said Jo. "And maybe not."

An idea leapt into my mind. "I think I'll borrow the mascot tonight, if no one minds," I said.

"What do you want it for?" asked Cal.

"Tell you tomorrow," I said.

103

| INNINGS OF .GLORY GARDENS........ | TOSS WON BY W.W.. WEATHER BRIGHT |

BATSMAN	RUNS SCORED	HOW OUT	BOWLER	SCORE
1 M. ROSE	1·1·1·1·1·2 >>	st GALE	MOHAMED	8
2 C. SEBASTIEN	1·2·2·1 >>	ct GALE	REIFER	6
3 C. DACOSTA	2·2 >>	bowled	MOHAMED	4
4 E. DAVIES	1 >>	ct SAMI	MOHAMED	1
5 H. KNIGHT	4·2·1·3·1·2·1·1·1·2·1·6	NOT	OUT	26
6 J. PADGETT	>>	bowled	MOHAMED	0
7 T. McCURDY	2·2·1·4·1·1 >>	ct CARTER	KATZ	11
8 T. VELLACOTT	1·1·1	NOT	OUT	3
9 F. ALLEN				
10 M. LEAR				
11 P. BENNETT				

FALL OF WICKETS											BYES	·1·1 ————	3	TOTAL EXTRAS	11
SCORE	1 15	2 23	3 27	4 30	5 30	6 58	7	8	9	10	L.BYES	·1	2	TOTAL 70	
BAT NO	2	3	4	1	6	7					WIDES	1·1·1	4	FOR	
											NO BALLS	1·1	2	WKTS	6

SCORE AT A GLANCE

BOWLER	BOWLING ANALYSIS @ NO BALL + WIDE													OVS	MDS	RUNS	WKT
	1	2	3	4	5	6	7	8	9	10	11	12	13				
1 L. GONSALVES	··· +1··	··· ·1·	··· ·21	+··· ·2·	X									4	0	10	0
2 W. REIFER	··1 ·2·	+·1 ·2·	W·· 0···	·+· 0···	X									4	0	10	1
3 Y. MOHAMED	W·	··· ···	·W· 2··	W3·2	X									4	1	8	4
4 L. KATZ	M	·· 1·	X	·4· 11··	1W· ··1	X								4	1	10	1
5 G. RUMBELLOW	·4· 21	1·2 1·3	1·1 ·1·	121 16										3·5	0	27	0
6																	
7																	
8																	
9																	

Chapter Thirteen

When I got home my mum told me Lizzy was out at Mave the Grave's. Perfect for my plan. I ran up to her bedroom and opened the window wide. Then I came down and had my supper.

It was getting dark when Lizzy came home.

"Oh, it's you," she said. "Hope you lost."

"No, we won," I said calmly without looking up. I could sense she was furious. "But I had a funny dream."

"Fancy that!" Lizzie said sneeringly.

"Yes," I said. "It was a sort of day dream. We were losing, you see, and I was batting and suddenly I had this vision of your 'Gatting' flying through the air to our rescue like Superman. It was weird – like I really saw him. And, you know, from that moment on we started to win."

Lizzie looked at me. "You're completely bonkers, Harry Knight!" she said. "Mavis always says cricket softens the brain." And then she went off to her room.

As the door shut I jumped up, grabbed 'Gatting' from my cricket bag and rushed out into the garden. I had to do it before she shut the bedroom window. I saw the light come on and heard her moving around in her bedroom. I positioned myself under the window, took aim and fired. A hole in one. 'Gatting' shot through the window. I waited.

There was a second's silence; then a huge scream. I smiled and ran back into the house and sat down in the same chair I'd been in before.

A few minutes later Lizzie burst into the kitchen holding the mascot. "Where'd you find that?" I asked before she could speak.

"You . . . you just threw him through my window, didn't you?" she said sharply but rather uncertainly.

"Me? Did you see me move out of this chair?" Well, it wasn't exactly a lie.

"Then how . . . " she began.

"Perhaps he flew in, like in my dream," I suggested. And I took the mascot from Lizzie. "Anyway, it's good to have him back. Perhaps we'll win our last League game now."

She stared at me and then at 'Gatting'. Finally she said, "Well I don't believe he flew in; someone must have thrown him. Probably the thief that took it in the first place." And she looked at 'Gatting', then at me, and back at 'Gatting' again.

I couldn't keep a straight face any longer.

"Sorry, Liz," I said. "But you should have seen your face just now."

She flew at me, laying into me with her little fists. "You did it. You're horrid and your friends are horrid and I hate you all."

After a bit she calmed down and I had a chance to tell her the story. When I told her about Gatting taking 'Gatting' home, she even smiled a bit.

"You mean he's been in Gatting's kennel all this time?"

"Yes."

"Poor old Gatting. I'll have to make another puppy for him," she said.

Yuk!

———————•———————

UNDER 13 LEAGUE RESULTS

Glory Gardens *beat* Wyckham Wanderers by four wickets
Old Courtiers *beat* Barmewell by 53 runs
Grunty Dyke *lost to* Mudlarks by five wickets

	P	W	Pts
Old Courtiers	4	4	40
Mudlarks	4	2	22*
Wyckham Wndrs	4	2	20
Glory Gardens	4	1	12*
Barmewell	4	1	10
Grunty Dyke	4	1	10

*No result in game between Mudlarks and Glory Gardens

"If we get ten points from the Grunty enquiry, we'll be equal second," said Erica.

"But no one can beat Old Courtiers now," said Marty.

"All the more reason to win when we play them," said Jo.

"Read all about it. Glory Gardens crush Champions!" said Frankie.

There weren't many of us at Nets on the Saturday after the Wyckham game. For a start it was half term and Azzie, Matthew and Jason had all gone away on holiday. Clive was doing the Knicker Rota and Jacky was still keeping out of the way. No one had heard from him since the trouble last Saturday.

"Perhaps we'll try the bowling machine," said Kiddo.

"Yeah!" said Frankie, leaping up and down doing the crazy war dance which means he's overexcited.

Kiddo got the machine out. It looks like a big pea shooter with a large can at one end. He set it on medium pace.

It was the first time we'd used the bowling machine. At first it was quite difficult to pick up the ball because the machine fires it at you when you aren't expecting it. But you get used to it.

Kiddo began by bowling well-pitched-up deliveries at me; then short-of-a-length ones. It's really useful because it helps you practise one particular stroke. I'm mainly a front-foot player but I know I've got to improve my back-foot shots. So for a quarter of an hour Kiddo sent down short-pitched balls on or just outside my leg stump. I had to decide whether to leg glance, hook, pull or play defensively. Jo videoed the whole session.

This is me leg glancing off the back foot. It's a useful shot – especially on a fast track. The important thing is to keep your bat close to your body. In fact, you play it just like a backward defensive stroke but at the last moment you turn your wrist and angle the ball down between square and fine-leg.

We spent ages watching the videos afterwards. Mack wanted to see everything he'd done in slow motion. "Oh heck, look at that shoulder," he kept saying. "No wonder I'm bowling down the leg." He analysed all his batting shots, too. "Look at that head in the air again" and "Now that's more like a forward defensive". I was beginning to realise that Mack's a bit of a perfectionist. He never stops watching and learning and asking questions.

After we'd been through the video twice Jo asked if we wanted to see the averages.

"Bet you can't guess who's the top wicket taker," she said.

"I can," said Tylan with a grin.

I knew Tylan had taken a lot of wickets but I was really surprised to see how many.

Bowling

	OVERS	RUNS	WCKTS	AVERAGE
Tylan	12.1	40	11	3.6
Hooker	14	29	6	4.8
Clive	5.4	14	2	7.0
Cal	10.5	38	4	9.5
Marty	11	36	3	12.0

Batting

	INNS	N/O	RUNS	AVERAGE
Azzie	2	1	59	59
Hooker	3	1	49	24.5
Clive	4	0	50	12.5
Cal	4	0	38	9.5
Erica	4	1	24	8

Just look at the performance of 'the great all-rounder'. Second in the batting *and* the bowling figures! But I was too modest to say anything, of course.

"I just can't believe Tylan's taken eleven wickets and Marty only three," said Frankie.

"It's because he gets to bowl at the rabbits all the time," said Marty.

"You can't argue with an average of 3.6," said Tylan with a smile.

"Eat your heart out, Shane Warne," said Mack.

"I can't understand why they don't thrash you all over the ground like we do in Nets," said Cal.

Tylan grinned, "I must be a natural pressure bowler," he said.

The door of the pavilion opened.

"I don't believe it," said Cal under his breath. We all turned and looked at Clive and Jacky who'd just walked in together like old mates.

"If it isn't those great pals, Tom and Jerry," said Frankie.

Clive looked uncomfortable and it was Jacky who spoke.

"We met at the stall," he said. "Er . . . well, if you must know I went looking for him."

It was only the second time Clive had done the Knicker Rota. He doesn't like it much; he says it's boring. But then Clive thinks everything's boring – even Nets.

"And I said it was time we stopped rowing," continued Jacky.

"And don't tell me Clive agreed," said Frankie.

"We think we should put the team first," said Jacky.

"Yeah," said Clive suddenly. It was the first word he'd spoken.

"Oh look, a flying pig," said Tylan.

"What about your brother?" I asked Jacky. "Does he know about this?"

"No. He'll kill me when he finds out. Anyway I'm available for the next game."

"That's a shame," said Frankie. "We've just dropped you both from the team."

"You're joking," said Clive.

"You're right. I am," said Frankie.

I didn't really believe it. I couldn't have been more surprised if Ohbert had scored a century. But I was very relieved to have Jacky back in the side. Mind you it was going to mean a big selection problem if both Jacky and Azzie wanted to play. But I decided I'd not worry about that for a few days. The next game was still twelve days away and Clive would probably upset someone else by then.

Half term went really quickly. I played cricket on the Rec every day except Wednesday when my mum took me and Lizzie to the seaside. Strangely Lizzie was suddenly being nice to me. She even bought me an ice cream. I wondered if she was feeling bad about the 'Gatting' thing. I mean she did go over the top a bit.

By Saturday it was warm again which was good because it was the first day of the Eastgate Priory Cricket Festival Week. The first team had an all day game and we finished Nets at 11.30 and stayed to watch.

They'd put up a big tent next to the pavilion for serving food and drink and the ground looked extra smart with all the boundary markers, flags flying and the sight-screens up.

The Priory won the toss and batted. Kiddo opened the batting, as usual. He brought Gatting over to us before he went out and asked us to look after him.

"Remember, don't rush things, Mr Johnstone," said Frankie. "Build your innings in fives and pick up those singles."

Kiddo laughed. "I hope you bring me luck, kiddoes. I'm a bit short of runs this year."

I'd never seen Kiddo batting in a match before. But the first thing I noticed was the bowling. It was fast. The Priory was playing a team called Croyland Crusaders and its opening bowlers were three times as fast as Win Reifer. The ball was flying around at head height.

"Fancy batting against this lot?" Mack asked Azzie.

"No trouble," said Azzie. "I'd have had twenty wides by now."

The first hour didn't go too well for the Priory. We lost four wickets and the score was only creeping along. But Kiddo was still there and he was looking better with every ball he faced. What I like about his batting is the time he has to decide whether to play back or forward. He doesn't move until the ball leaves the bowler's hand. And he gets everything behind it when he's playing defensively. And when he goes on the attack, it's all timing and footwork.

"Jeez, I wish I could do that," said Mack, as a perfect cover drive bounced over the rope. "He hardly hits it and it goes like a rocket."

"Fifty up," shouted Jo. She and Ohbert had just arrived from the pavilion with a trayful of drinks and a bowl of water for Gatting. He drank the water and then wolfed down Cal's lemonade when he wasn't looking.

"We're having tea in the tent on Thursday," said Jo.

"Yes," said Ohbert. "It's because it's Cricket Week. Did you know that?"

"Oh, so that's why there's a big sign over the gate saying 'Eastgate Priory Cricket Week'," said Tylan.

"And it explains why there's a cricket match every day this week," said Frankie. "Cricket Week! That's a good name for it, isn't it, Ohbert?"

"Yes," said Ohbert.

Jo said our game against Old Courtiers was in the special Cricket Week programme. She showed us it.

Glory Gardens v Old Courtiers
Final Game in the North County Under Thirteen League.

"See, they've called us 'Glory Gardens' and not 'Eastgate Priory'," said Jo proudly. It was she who'd insisted we kept the name Glory Gardens right at the beginning.

"We're having tea between innings on Thursday," she added. "And there'll be a big crowd because there's a barbecue after the . . ." She broke off as an enormous six from a Kiddo hook flew inches over Ohbert's head.

Mack was standing just behind Ohbert and he took a great

catch and threw the ball all the way back to the wicket-keeper. Everyone clapped Kiddo.

"Great shot," shouted Frankie. "You know what, kiddoes, I think this lad can bat a bit. I'd be surprised if he hasn't played before."

We all laughed at Frankie's impersonation.

"Oh but, you sound just like Kiddo," said Ohbert. Frankie threw a lemonade can at him.

A four from Kiddo brought up his 50. The Priory were on 81 for 4. His first 50 had been chanceless. He'd picked up the singles and thumped the bad balls. It had taken him 25 overs or just over an hour and a half. But what came next was breathtaking. Not that he went wild or anything, but he played shots all round the wicket and completely destroyed the bowling.

The Crusaders brought back the opening quickies to try and slow him down and Kiddo took eighteen off one over with three consecutive fours and a six. The six was a huge cut drive played deliberately in the air through cover-point. I'd only ever seen Ian Botham play the shot before and that was on video. It was amazing. The ball never rose more than a couple of metres off the ground and it went like a bullet. It just missed an old man on the boundary and he nearly fell out of his deck chair as the ball whizzed past his ear.

Kiddo's 100 came in the last over before lunch. A perfect on drive for four took him to exactly 100. Jo said the second 50 had come off 30 balls. Eastgate Priory were 149 for four at lunch.

Everyone on the ground clapped Kiddo in. Gatting had been asleep but even he seemed to know something special had happened and he walked over and gave Kiddo one of his big, smelly licks. We weren't too sorry to see the back of Gatting because all that lemonade had had a nasty effect on his digestion. We all blamed Tylan's feet for the smell until Frankie realised it was the dog.

We had sausages and hamburgers for lunch. And in the

afternoon The Priory went on to score 268. Kiddo was out caught on the boundary for 135. They bowled the Crusaders out for 174; Dave Wing took five for 48.

"We've got to win on Thursday," said Jo as we walked home. "We can't let everyone see that Glory Gardens aren't good enough for The Priory."

"Some hope against Old Courtiers," said Marty. "They're unbeaten."

"You wait till Thursday," said Mack. "They won't know what's hit them."

Chapter Fourteen

Lizzy was still being unusually friendly.

When I told her we were having tea and a barbecue at the game on Thursday, she said, "Oh great, I'll make a huge jelly and some cakes, if you like."

"You don't need to do that," I said weakly. She'd only made a jelly once before and you could hardly get your spoon in it. It just lay there and set; it was like trying to attack a balloon that wouldn't burst.

"Oh, it's no trouble," said Lizzie.

"Well, er . . . great," I said. "Just a small one."

We didn't know much about Old Courtiers except that they were good. Liam Katz told me they had three or four excellent batsmen and a very accurate bowling attack.

"We lost because they tied our batsmen down," he said. Of course, he'd got a terrible umpiring decision and it was never lbw in a million years.

The Selection Committee, Marty, Jo and myself, decided unanimously to pick our strongest team. Even Jo admitted we had to play Mack instead of Ohbert this time.

Matthew Rose	Mack McCurdy
Cal Sebastien	Tylan Vellacott
Azzie Nazar	Frankie Allen
Clive da Costa	Jacky Gunn
Erica Davies	Marty Lear
Hooker Knight	

Jason made it easier for us by volunteering to stand down. He hasn't had a good season with the bat but it would have been hard to drop him because he's one of the regulars and Mack has only played one game for us. I think Jason has lost interest in cricket a bit this year. He seems to spend all his spare time playing chess these days and I wasn't too surprised when he said he wouldn't really mind missing a game.

I felt more sorry for Ohbert. Even he must know he's the worst cricketer in the world but, in a funny way, I think he loves playing as much as any of us. You can't exactly be sure with Ohbert but I'd say he was really unhappy about being dropped. He hardly said a word to anyone at school all week and he had his Walkman turned up extra loud.

He was at the ground on Thursday evening, still looking sick as a parrot. Well, more like a crow really. He was wearing black jeans, a slimy-black tee-shirt that looked as if it had been dipped in engine oil and a bright yellow baseball cap – with, of course, the Walkman on top.

"Hey, Ohbert," said Frankie. "You going to a funeral?"

Ohbert just grunted and when Frankie gave him a friendly slap on the back he turned on him angrily and said, "I hope you drop ten catches, Frankie Allen." Frankie left him alone. It wasn't like Ohbert at all.

The Cricket Week marquee looked amazing. In the centre were two large tables heaped with food. There were sausages on sticks and legs of chicken and tarts and pies, scones with jam and cream, chocolate cakes and fresh strawberries. In the middle of one of the tables stood an enormous red jelly. It looked all right but I gave it a prod with my finger and it hardly moved. Must be Lizzie's, I thought.

"Keep your hands off the food, Harry Knight," said a voice behind me. It was Lizzie; Mave the Grave was with her.

"Sorry, Liz," I said. "Er . . . I was just admiring your jelly."

"Brilliant, isn't it?" she said. "I borrowed a mould from Mavis's mum. That's why it's so big."

"Isn't it," I said. It sat there like a huge marker buoy in the middle of a sea of delicious food. It didn't even wobble.

I was saved from Lizzie and the Ten-Ton-Jelly by Marty.

"Cal's going to be half an hour late," he said. "His mum's just remembered he's got a dentist's appointment after school and she says he's got to go. He's really pleased."

I wasn't overjoyed either. "I suppose Erica can open the batting," I said. "And if we're fielding, Jason can sub."

"He's not here," said Marty.

"Then ask Ohbert, though I don't suppose he's brought his kit."

Old Courtiers' skipper was called Vaughan. He never stopped smiling while we were tossing up. That's what it must be like to captain a team that wins everything, I thought. He won the toss, too, and did what I'd have done . . . bat. The Priory pitch had never looked better. 'A batsman's dream' is what Vaughan called it.

Ohbert was really pleased to be fielding. He'd brought his kit along fortunately, so he didn't have to play in black. "I didn't mean that about dropping catches," he said to Frankie.

"Oh that's a relief," said Frankie.

I set an attacking field for Marty with a slip and a squarish gully.

Things started well for us – a wicket in the first over. Their opener tried an ambitious cut shot before he'd got his eye in and chopped the ball on to his stumps.

The fielding was really keen. Mack was brilliant as usual and his enthusiasm rubbed off on everyone else. Ohbert was amazing. He was running around like a wind-up toy and he made two brilliant stops at square-leg. Marty and Jacky both bowled a good line and Marty seemed to have got his run-up right and he was getting an extra yard of pace.

"First time I've seen him hit his straps," said Mack.

I thought I knew what he meant but I wasn't sure. I suppose it means something in Australia.

Frankie gave away a couple of byes – he was having trouble with the pace of the ball off the wicket.

Marty has a good action for a fast bowler. Notice the high left knee as he comes into the delivery stride. As he releases the ball his weight is on the braced left leg.

"Get your fat body behind it," snarled Marty after Frankie let one through his legs. Marty always bowls better when he's a bit wound up.

Six overs had gone and they were 19 for one. Their captain, Vaughan was playing the bowling well, though he had a bit of luck with an edge off Marty that didn't quite carry to Azzie at slip. I decided to take Marty off, so I could bring him back for a flat-out over later on if things started going wrong. And I turned to Tylan – the man in form.

His first ball was a rank long-hop which Vaughan swung over square-leg. It looked like a four the moment it left the bat. But Ohbert had other ideas. He turned and chased after the ball like a hyena closing in on its prey. It even seemed for a moment that he might win the race to the boundary. But no, the ball bounced over the rope just in front of the marquee. And seconds later, Ohbert followed it.

"Oh no!" said Frankie putting his hands over his eyes.

Ohbert tried desperately to stop. There was the marquee looming up in front of him. It seemed he had nowhere to go. Suddenly he swerved, caught his foot on a tent peg and took off, head first, straight through the entrance of the marquee. "OOOOOOOHAAAAIIEEE!" CRASH!

We all raced over to see what had happened. It was carnage! In the centre of the marquee, where the food tables had been, was Ohbert. He was spread out like a crashed jumbo in the middle of the remains of our tea. One of the tables had collapsed under him. Strawberries and cream were splattered all over the floor and the sides of the tent. And where Ohbert's head should have been there was an enormous squashed, red blob.

Slowly he rose.

"The Creature from the Red Lagoon," said Frankie.

"My jelly!" screamed Lizzie.

"Are you all right, Ohbert?" asked Jo.

"Oh but . . . I think so," said the red blob.

"Come on, Ohbert," said Tylan. "We're playing cricket. It's not tea time yet."

Everyone laughed except Lizzie who was still staring at the remains of her jelly.

"At least it softened his landing," I said to her.

"Your stupid cricket team always wrecks everything," she said. And she stormed out of the tent with Mave the Grave in grim pursuit.

Cal arrived just in time to see Ohbert disappearing for an early bath and we continued the game.

Frankie had grabbed a pocketful of sausages. He offered me one. "Might as well have tea now. There won't be much later unless we scrape it off the tent."

The rest of Tylan's over wasn't much better than his first

ball. His length was all over the place and Old Courtiers took full advantage. Twelve runs came off the over.

"Sorry, Hooker," said Tylan as he chucked me the ball. "I can't seem to get the flight right – especially when I bowl the googly."

"But you don't bowl googlies!"

"Yes I do. I persuaded Wingy to teach me."

"Then just forget what he told you and bowl like you used to," I said. "Or I'll take you off."

Jacky helped us fight back with a sharp caught and bowled off a full-blooded drive. Clive gave him a slap on the back and said, "Well bowled."

Tylan's next over was a bit better – though it still cost us seven runs. I half decided to take him off but I kept thinking about all the wickets he had taken this year. A couple of quick wickets and we'd be on top.

Erica came on at Jacky's end and she was straight into her usual line and length. At the half way stage they were 44 for two. No one was on top yet, but I knew the crunch would come in the next five overs. It came immediately.

In this third over Tylan lost it completely. It started with a wide about 2 metres down the leg side. That was followed by a full toss and a wide over the batsman's head which Frankie did well to reach.

"I think he's got the yips," said Mack.

"Yes," I said. It seemed a good word for the way Tylan was bowling but I didn't know what it meant.

A long hop went for four and then Tylan was even 'no-balled' for overstepping the bowling crease. He looked wretched and I felt really sorry for him. With three wides and a no ball it seemed the over would never end. When it did Old Courtiers had eighteen more runs and Tylan was nearly in tears.

"Thanks, Ty," I said. "Take a break."

"Sorry," he said and walked off into the outfield shaking his head.

"Never mind, Ty," said Frankie. "Even Shane Warne bowls rubbish sometimes."

Fortunately Erica wasn't having an off day. She sent down a perfect over – every ball on the stumps. Finally the batsman lost patience and took a wild swing. He top-edged to Matthew at mid-on and he took a good catch.

I came on at Tylan's end. I knew, with seven wickets left, that Old Courtiers would press home the attack. Vaughan had 34 and he'd already knocked five boundaries. I set a really defensive field with five on the off-side and four on the leg.

The plan worked for a couple of overs thanks to Erica, Mack and Cal who were brilliant in the covers. One spectacular dive from Mack saved a certain four and his instant throw was right over the stumps. Frankie had the bails off in a flash and I was sure it was a run out. But Old Sid gave the batsman the benefit of the doubt – I suppose it must have been quite close.

Erica got one to cut in a bit, which was almost impossible on this pitch but Frankie dropped the catch off the inside edge. It wasn't an expensive drop because she got the same batsman plumb lbw a couple of balls later.

"Thanks Erica," said Frankie. "I'd have been a bit sick if he'd gone on to make 50."

"You'll be a bit sick paying me 50p," said Cal.

"Blame Ohbert," said Frankie. "He's put a spell on me."

Erica ended her four overs with two for 11 – that was brilliant because thanks to Tylan, we'd been under the cosh.

Four overs left and they had 79 on the board. I got the next wicket with a straight yorker. Then I must have relaxed a bit and I was struck for two consecutive fours by the incoming batsman – both dragged from outside off-stump and swung over mid-wicket.

I decided to bring back Marty against the slogger.

"He can only play on the leg side," said Marty. "So let's have six fielders out on the boundary and keep our fingers crossed."

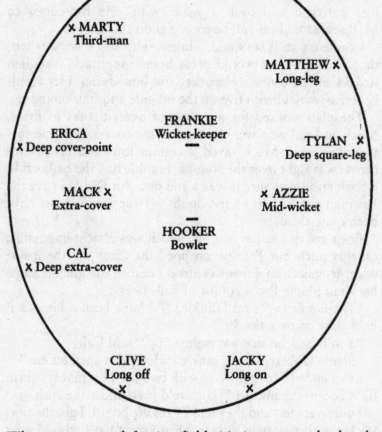

× MARTY
Third-man

MATTHEW ×
Long-leg

FRANKIE
Wicket-keeper

ERICA
× Deep cover-point

TYLAN ×
Deep square-leg

MACK ×
Extra-cover

× AZZIE
Mid-wicket

HOOKER
Bowler

CAL
× Deep extra-cover

CLIVE
Long off
×

JACKY
Long on
×

When you set a defensive field, it's important the bowler bowls to the field. My line must be a full length on or just out-side off-stump. The two quickest fielders, Mack and Azzie have the job of cutting off the short singles. The best catchers in the team, Erica, Clive, Cal and Jacky are in the most likely places for the ball to be hit in the air.

It didn't look a very good plan when two more fours shot through the gap between Mack at deep square-leg and Erica on the mid-wicket boundary. The slogger was using his bat like a baseball player would – but he had a wonderful eye for the ball. To make things worse Frankie dropped another sharp chance.

"That's a quid," said Cal, "but I'll let you off if you catch one."

"Done," said Frankie.

"Fat chance," said Marty gloomily.

With the last ball of the over Marty got his man. It looked as if the catch was going to drop short of Mack but he raced in all of fifteen metres to take it on the run.

98 for six with two overs to go. I now had the job of bowling to Vaughan who was on 42. I hit him on the pads but it was outside off-stump. He pulled an awful long hop for four to bring up the 100. I beat him outside the off-stump. He drove me into the covers for two. Then I got one to move away a touch and he tried to drive it on the up. The ball took the thinnest edge and flew to Frankie who fumbled it, knocked it up, fumbled and caught it on the second rebound.

"You lucky devil," said Cal.

"Just teasing," said Frankie with a grin.

We clapped Vaughan to the pavilion. He'd scored 48 out of 104.

My last ball was a corker. It was the off-cutter and it did for the new batsman through the gate, knocking out his off-stump.

Cal bowled the last over. He kept them down to only another six runs. A lightning run out on the last ball by Mack – who else – gave us our ninth wicket.

As we walked in for tea, I realised we'd have to score a record 111 to win.

HOME TEAM GLORY GARDENS **V** OLD COURTIERS **AWAY TEAM**
AT EASTGATE PRIORY **DATE** JUNE 9TH.

INNINGS OF OLD COURTIERS **TOSS WON BY** O.C. **WEATHER** SUNNY.

BATSMAN	RUNS SCORED	HOW OUT	BOWLER	SCORE
1 H.CARLTON	1.2.1.1.1.2	c & b	GUNN	8
2 J.STAEDTLER	1.	bowled	LEAR	1
3 V.MATTIS	1.2.1.1.4.1.4.1.1.2.4.4.2.4.1.1. 1.2.1.1.1.4.2	ct ALLEN	KNIGHT	48
4 M.JARMAN	1.1.2.1.1.2	ct ROSE	DAVIES	8
5 P.RAMESH	1.1.1.1.2	lbw	DAVIES	6
6 W.RUSSELL	1.	bowled	KNIGHT	1
7 G.PRICE	4.4.1.4.4	ct McCURDY	LEAR	17
8 B.MUKHI	2.1.2	RUN	OUT	5
9 O.LANGEY		bowled	KNIGHT	0
10 W.WEEKES		NOT	OUT	0
11 D.McGINTY				

FALL OF WICKETS

	1	2	3	4	5	6	7	8	9	10
SCORE	3	33	64	78	79	98	104	104	110	
BAT NO	2	1	4	5	6	7	3	9	8	

BYES	1.2.1.1	5
L BYES	1.1.1.1.1.1	7
WIDES	1.1.1	3
NO BALLS	1.	1

TOTAL EXTRAS 16
TOTAL 110
FOR WKTS 9

SCORE AT A GLANCE

BOWLER	BOWLING ANALYSIS · NO BALL + WIDE													OVS	MDS	RUNS	WKT
	1	2	3	4	5	6	7	8	9	10	11	12	13				
1 M.LEAR	..iW	M	2.i	X	4.4 ..W									4	1	13	2
2 J.GUNN	... 2.i	.ii .i.	ii. W.i	X										4	0	10	1
3 T.VELLACOTT	412 .41	.. 1W.. 4.42i	.1+4 2i.	X										3	0	37	0
4 E.DAVIES	..2 ..1	1W.	1.2 1.. W.i	X										4	1	11	2
5 H.KNIGHT	..1. .11	.11 W.4. 4.1 2iW	X											4	0	22	3
6 C.SEBASTIEN	.2i 2.													1	0	5	0
7																	
8																	
9																	

Chapter Fifteen

Tea wasn't too bad after all. Ohbert hadn't flattened everything. The sausages and the strawberries had survived. And the scones and cream. As for Ohbert, he'd managed to wash off all the jelly and he was quite cheerful about his nose dive.

"We want an action replay," said Tylan. "Show us how you did it, Ohbert."

"Do you usually eat jelly like that, Ohbert?" said Frankie.

There was no sign of Lizzie and The Grave. But it wasn't long before I discovered why. I found the remains of the jelly in my kit bag. They had carefully squeezed it into my socks and batting gloves and completely filled my protective box with it. It was disgusting but everyone else thought it was very funny.

It's difficult to concentrate on going out to score a big total when you've got jelly in your box and batting gloves.

What was certain was that at least one, and probably two players would have to make a big score. A lot was going to depend on Azzie or Clive or me.

So much for plans!

Matthew and Cal were about to go out to bat when Clive fainted. He'd been very quiet throughout the game and he hadn't had any tea. I'd noticed him turn quite green when he saw Frankie's plate stacked with sausages, strawberries, cakes and an enormous slice of ham and egg pie. He fainted on top of the team kit bag. Jacky and Marty picked him up and laid him flat on the floor and I went to fetch Kiddo.

When we came back Clive was sitting up.

"We used Tylan's socks to bring him round," said Frankie.

"Feeling okay, kiddo?" asked Kiddo.

"Yeah," said Clive feebly.

"Well you can't blame it on Lizzie's jelly," said Frankie. "Ohbert didn't leave him any."

"You're the one who ought to be sick, you great gannet," said Cal.

Clive was looking a bit better but Kiddo said he should lie down and it would probably be better if he didn't bat. Clive tried to argue but anyone could see he wasn't really in a fit state.

Whatever you may say about Glory Gardens, it's never a dull team to play for.

The important thing now was to get the innings off to a solid start. Liam Katz had been right about their bowling; it was tight and quick. Vaughan Mattis, their captain, was quite sharp but he also had a well-disguised change of pace. He very nearly got Matthew with his slower ball.

Matthew and Cal battled away but the runs were coming too slowly. After six overs we had only 14 on the board. Cal was playing and missing a lot and he was getting more and more frustrated. Finally he played a horrible shot with his head in the air and his middle stump was flattened.

Azzie came in and, after a brief look at the bowling, he hit two glorious 4s, one through mid-off and the other cracked through the covers.

"Azzie, Azzie," chanted Frankie. "Show them, my man."

If Azzie stayed for just twenty minutes we'd be back in the hunt. But it wasn't to be. He went to hit one on the up and got a thick inside edge straight down mid-wicket's throat.

I was starting to get worried. With Matthew and Erica at the wicket I thought we'd struggle to keep up with the run rate. But, as usual, Erica got it about right. She kept the score-board moving with singles and twos.

Erica plays a delicate cut for two. You can play this shot to a short-of-a-length ball just outside off-stump. Erica's head is right over the ball and she plays the shot with a final flick downwards with the wrists.

Erica's very good at playing the ball into the gaps in the field. There was a big gap on the off-side because third-man was fine. She found it with a lovely cut.

After ten overs we still had only 36 on the board but at least we hadn't lost any more wickets. They now had two spinners on and I knew if we were going to win we had to chance it against them. Erica fell to a good catch at square-leg and I was in. I swung my first ball away for two and I was relieved to see that there wasn't a lot of turn in the pitch.

"Keep playing straight," I said to Matthew. "We can still win this if we don't panic."

"Me panic?" said Matthew calmly.

I stepped back to the next one and pulled a short ball from the off-spinner for four. That was better.

Another four came off a real heave – what Kiddo calls a

cow shot – over mid-wicket. Then I tried to repeat the shot, taking a step down the track and missed completely. The keeper had the bails off before I could turn.

"Go for it, Mack," I said as we passed each other.

He grinned broadly. "No worry, skip. Death or glory."

He went for it all right. Nine runs came off the next over – though to be fair Matthew scored four of them.

"I don't believe it," said Frankie. "Matthew's hitting the ball off the square."

"He's got 23," said Jo.

"Don't knock him," said Cal. "He's holding the side together."

With his spinners bowled out, Vaughan went back to an all seam attack and Mack immediately holed out at mid-on.

Frankie joined Matthew and instantly there was a disaster. Matthew called a quick leg-bye and pulled up suddenly at the end of the run. He'd gone over on his ankle in a rough patch at the edge of the strip and, after hobbling around for a few moments, he decided he'd have to have a runner.

Mack had still got his pads on. "I'll do it," he said. "Should be fun."

"Fun?" said Cal. "Frankie's a liability at the best of times. There's bound to be a run out."

"I can't watch," said Marty.

Matthew was on strike. He pushed one out on the off-side and called for a run. He set off, then remembered Mack was running for him and stopped. So Frankie stopped, too. "Run!" screamed Mack and everyone on the Glory Gardens bench, and Frankie lumbered off again and made it by a whisker.

As usual Frankie then tried to win it in fours. He got enough bat on the ball to score runs off two enormous heaves but the end came with his third wild swing which he missed completely. He was plumb in front when the ball cannoned into his pads.

Tylan was unlucky to get a beauty – it would have claimed

a much better batsman than him. Jacky Gunn avoided one horrible run out mix up but then the inevitable happened. Jacky called Mack for an impossible single, stopped and suddenly shouted, "No." Mack turned and slipped and the throw to the bowler's end beat him easily. It was a sad end to Matthew's innings and he limped off with his arm round Mack who was carrying both bats. He'd scored 31.

With him gone our last chance had probably disappeared, too. We now needed 12 to win off nine balls. Jacky and Marty scratched around for another six nail-biting runs and then Marty, too was run out. Jacky called him through for a leg-bye but he hesitated and looked round to see where the ball had gone. By the time he turned and ran he had no chance of beating the throw to the bowler's end. It was the second run out Jacky had been involved in – though this one wasn't his fault.

So that was it. We'd got within five runs of Old Courtiers' total and had run out of batsmen.

Or had we?

Chapter Sixteen

Suddenly a pale-looking Clive appeared on the pavilion steps. He looked very shaky but he was wearing his pads.

"Three balls left," said Jo as he passed us. "Six to win."

"Good luck, Clive," said Matt.

Clive smiled weakly.

They'd crossed so Jacky had the strike. Our best chance was for Clive to get down the other end. Jacky and Clive had a brief chat in the middle.

Jacky swung at the ball. Missed. Almost before it reached the keeper Clive was through for the single. He leaned on his bat at the striker's end and gasped for breath. 106 for 9. Five to win.

Clive didn't bother to take guard. He got a well-pitched-up ball on his wicket and drove it. It went off the toe of the bat to the left of the bowler. It was only a single because long-on was coming in fast. But no, Jacky was running like the wind and he just made the second run before the throw came in.

Three to win. The last ball and Clive on strike. He looked round the field. Vaughan took ages to organise his field. He kept moving fielders to the left and to the right. In the end every one of them was on the boundary. Five on the leg side. Four on the off. Clive staggered slightly and wiped his forehead with his sleeve. He looked round; there weren't many gaps. His best chance was either behind square on the leg side or in front of cover-point. The off-side boundary was closer.

At last in came the bowler. It was a good length ball on leg stump. Clive took a step back and swung through the ball. It was the perfect shot. The ball screamed off his bat and rocketed between cover-point and extra-cover. A great cheer went up as it bounced over the rope.

Glory Gardens went wild. Frankie jumped on the scorers' table and it collapsed under him. Jo hit him with her scorebook. In the middle Clive and Jacky had their arms round each other's shoulders like long-lost friends. Clive still looked rotten but he had a big grin on his face.

Clive picks his spot with this typical 'one day' shot to a ball on leg stump.

"Well batted, mate," said Vaughan as I walked out to shake hands with him. "I thought we were through you. What's the idea keeping your best batsman till last?"

I told him Clive had been ill.

"He's never our best batsman," said Jacky slapping Clive on the back. "Only equal best."

"Not sure about that," said Clive modestly. But then he *was* ill.

Mack and Cal rushed up and carried Clive shoulder high to the pavilion. It was brilliant. The biggest crowd we'd ever had and everyone was clapping and cheering.

"Well done, kiddoes. Best match of the week," said Kiddo.

"What do you expect from the best team," said Frankie.

"Here's the Man of the Match," said Kiddo as Matthew limped towards us and then blushed bright red.

"And here's the winner of the Champagne Moment," said Frankie. "Ohbert Bennett for his daring Jelly Flop."

"Oh, I nearly forgot the good news," said Kiddo. "You've got another ten points for beating Grunty Dyke."

"I don't believe it," said Marty.

"Won't the Hoggs be pig sick," said Frankie.

"That means we're second in the League with 32 points to old Courtiers' 40," said Jo.

Not a bad season after all, I thought.

INNINGS OF GLORY GARDENS | TOSS WON BY O.C. | WEATHER SUNNY

BATSMAN	RUNS SCORED	HOW OUT	BOWLER	SCORE
1 M. ROSE	1.1.1.1.1.1.1.2.1.1.2.1.1.1.2.1.2.1 1.2.1.1.2.1	RUN	OUT	31
2 C. SEBASTIEN	2.2.1.1.1	bowled	MATTIS	7
3 A. NAZAR	4.4.2	ct PRICE	WEEKES	10
4 E. DAVIES	1.2.2.1.1.3	ct RUSSELL	RAMESH	10
5 H. KNIGHT	2.4.1.3.4.2	st CARLTON	JARMAN	16
6 T. McCURDY	2.2.3.2	ct MATTIS	McGINTY	9
7 F. ALLEN	2.2	lbw	RUSSELL	4
8 T. VELLACOTT	2.	bowled	RUSSELL	2
9 J. GUNN	2.2.1.1.1	NOT	OUT	7
10 M. LEAR	1.1.	RUN	OUT	2
11 C. DA COSTA	2.4	NOT	OUT	6

FALL OF WICKETS											BYES	1.1.	2	TOTAL EXTRAS	8
SCORE	14	25	47	68	82	91	94	99	105	10	L BYES	1.1.1.1	4	TOTAL FOR	112
	1	2	3	4	5	6	7	8	9		WIDES	1.	1		
BAT NO	2	3	4	5	6	7	8	1	10		NO BALLS	1.	1	WKTS	9

SCORE AT A GLANCE

BOWLING ANALYSIS ⊙ NO BALL + WIDE

BOWLER	1	2	3	4	5	6	7	8	9	10	11	12	13	OVS	MDS	RUNS	WKT
1 V. MATTIS	.·.1	|M|	.¦.1.	W.. .44	✕									4	1	11	1
2 W. WEEKES	.2.	·2. 0.1.1.	1..	..1 2W.	✕									4	0	11	1
3 M. JARMAN	.1 .12	2.1. 3.1	·1. 4.11	4.2W .22	✕									4	0	29	1
4 P. RAMESH	.21 11	.2. W2.	.13 .2.	1.3 212	✕									4	0	25	1
5 D. McGINTY	1W. 212	21. 211												2	0	13	1
6 W. RUSSELL	12W. 2W.11	11. 2.24												2	0	17	2
7																	
8																	
9																	

FINAL LEAGUE TABLE

	PLAY	WON	LOST	POINTS
Old Courtiers	5	4	1	40
Glory Gardens	5	3	1	32*
Mudlarks	5	3	1	32*
Barmewell	5	2	3	20
Wyckham Wanderers	5	2	3	20
Grunty Dyke	5	0	5	0

Results

Glory Gardens *beat* **Old Courtiers** by one wicket
Wyckham Wanderers *lost to* **Mudlarks** by 6 runs
Barmewell *beat* **Grunty Dyke** by 28 runs

*The game between Mudlarks and Glory Gardens ended in no result.

Batting Averages

	INN	N/O	RUNS	S/R	H/S	AVERAGE
Azzie	3	1	69	108	53*	34.5
Hooker	4	1	68	86	26*	22.7
Clive	5	1	56	86	22	14.0
Matthew	5	0	47	31	31	9.4
Cal	5	0	45	49	14	9.0
Erica	5	1	34	47	17	8.5

Scoring Rate (S/R) is based on the average number of runs scored per 100 balls. So Azzie's scoring rate is better than a run a ball.

Highest score: Azzie, 53* v Mudlarks
Highest partnership: Azzie and Cal, 50 v Mudlarks
Minimum qualification, 30 runs.

Bowling Averages

	OVERS	MDN	RUNS	WKTS	S/RATE	ECON	BB	AVERAGE
Hooker	18	2	51	9	12.0	2.8	3/22	5.7
Tylan	15.1	0	79	11	8.3	5.2	3/5	7.2
Erica	13.3	1	39	4	20.3	2.9	2/11	9.8
Marty	15	1	49	5	18.0	3.3	2/13	9.8
Cal	11.5	1	41	4	17.8	3.6	2/14	10.3
Jacky	14	0	62	3	28.0	4.4	2/15	21.0

Strike Rate (S/Rate) shows that Hooker takes a wicket every 12 balls. Economy Rate (Econ) is the average number of runs given away each over.

	WKTS	BOWLED	CAUGHT	LBW	STUMPED
Hooker	9	6	3	0	0
Tylan	11	5	5	1	0
Erica	4	0	2	2	0
Marty	5	2	3	0	0
Cal	4	2	2	0	0
Jacky	3	1	2	0	0

Best bowling: Tylan, 3/5 v Wyckham Wanderers

Minimum qualification, 10 overs

Catching

	CAUGHT	DROPPED	AGGREGATE
Azzie	2	0	+2
Erica	2	1	+1
Tylan	2	1	+1
Hooker	1	0	+1
Jason	1	0	+1
Ohbert	1	0	+1
Mack	1	0	+1
Matthew	1	0	+1
Cal	2	2	0
Jacky	1	1	0
Frankie	4	5	-1
Marty	0	1	-1

CRICKET COMMENTARY

crease

At each end of the wicket the crease is marked out in white paint like this:

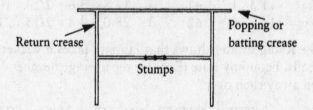

Return crease

Popping or batting crease

Stumps

The batsman is 'in his ground' when his bat or either foot are behind the batting or 'popping' crease. He can only be given out 'stumped' or 'run out' if he is outside the crease.

The bowler must not put his front foot down beyond the popping crease when he bowls. And his back foot must be inside the return crease. If he breaks these rules the umpire will call a 'no ball'.

leg side/ off-side

The cricket pitch is divided down the middle. Everything on the side of the batsman's legs is called the 'leg side' or 'on side' and the other side is called the 'off-side'.

Remember, when a left-handed bat is batting, his legs are on the other side. So leg side and off-side switch round.

leg stump

Three stumps and two bails make up each wicket. The 'leg stump' is on the same side as the batsman's legs. Next to it is the 'middle stump' and then the 'off-stump'.

off/on side	See **leg side**
off-stump	See **leg stump**
pitch	The 'pitch' is the area between the two wickets. It is 22 yards long from wicket to wicket (although it's usually 20 yards for Under 11s and 21 yards for Under 13s). The grass on the pitch is closely mown and rolled flat. Just to make things confusing, sometimes the whole ground is called a 'cricket pitch'.
square	The area in the centre of the ground where the strips are.
strip	Another name for the pitch. They are called strips because there are several pitches side by side on the square. A different one is used for each match.
track	Another name for the pitch or strip.
wicket	'Wicket' means two things, so it can sometimes confuse people. 1 The stumps and bails at each end of the pitch. The batsman defends his wicket. 2 The pitch itself. So you can talk about a hard wicket or a turning wicket (if it's taking spin).

BATTING

attacking strokes	The attacking strokes in cricket all have names. There are forward strokes (played off the front foot) and backward strokes (played off the back foot). The drawing shows where

the different strokes are played around the wicket.

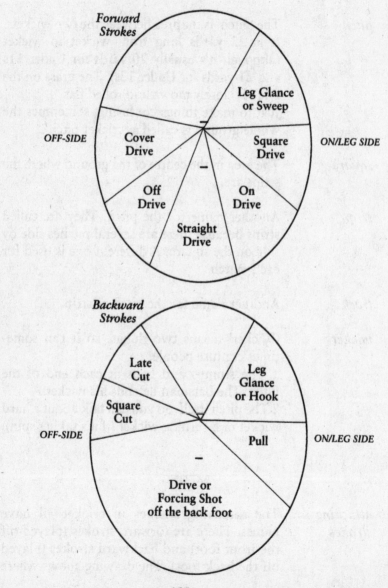

Forward Strokes

Leg Glance or Sweep

Cover Drive

Square Drive

OFF-SIDE

ON/LEG SIDE

Off Drive

On Drive

Straight Drive

Backward Strokes

Late Cut

Leg Glance or Hook

Square Cut

OFF-SIDE

ON/LEG SIDE

Pull

Drive or Forcing Shot off the back foot

backing up	As the bowler bowls, the non-striking batsman should start moving down the wicket to be ready to run a quick single. This is called 'backing up'.
bye	If the ball goes past the bat and the keeper misses it, the batsmen can run a 'bye'. If it hits the batsman's pad or any part of his body (apart from his glove), the run is called a 'leg-bye'. Byes and leg-byes are put in the 'Extras' column in the scorebook. They are not credited to the batsman or scored against the bowler's analysis. This is how an umpire will signal a bye and leg-bye.

Bye

Leg-bye

centre	See **guard**
cow shot	When the batsman swings across the line of a delivery, aiming towards mid-wicket, it is often called a 'cow shot'.

defensive strokes	There are basically two defensive shots: the 'forward defensive', played off the front foot and the 'backward defensive' played off the back foot
duck	When a batsman is out before scoring any runs it's called a 'duck'. If he's out first ball for nought it's a 'golden duck'.
gate	If a batsman is bowled after the ball has passed between his bat and pads it is sometimes described as being bowled 'through the gate'.
hit wicket	If the batsman knocks off a bail with his bat or any part of his body when the ball is in play, he is out 'hit wicket'.
lbw	Means leg before wicket. In fact a batsman can be given out lbw if the ball hits any part of his body and the umpire thinks it would have hit the stumps. There are two important extra things to remember about lbw: 1 If the ball pitches outside the leg stump and hits the batsman's pads it's not out – even if the ball would have hit the stumps. 2 If the ball pitches outside the off-stump and hits the pad outside the line, it's not out if the batsman is playing a shot. If he's not playing a shot he can still be given out.
guard	When you go in to bat the first thing you do is to 'take your guard'. You hold your bat sideways in front of the stumps and ask the

umpire to give you a guard. He'll show you which way to move the bat until it's in the right position.

The usual guards are 'leg stump' (sometimes called '1'); 'middle and leg' ('2') and 'centre' or 'middle' ('3').

innings
This means a batsman's stay at the wicket. 'It was the best *innings* I'd seen Azzie play.'
But it can also mean the batting score of the whole team. 'In their first *innings* England scored 360.'

knock
Another word for a batsman's innings.

leg-bye
See **bye**

*middle/
middle and leg*
See **guard**

out
There are six common ways of a batsman being given out in cricket: bowled, caught, lbw, hit wicket, run out and stumped. Then there are a few rare ones like handled the ball and hit the ball twice. When the fielding side thinks the batsman is out they must appeal (usually a shout of "Owzthat"). If the umpire considers the batsman is out, he will signal 'out' like this:

play *forward/back*	You play forward by moving your front foot down the wicket towards the bowler as you play the ball. You play back by putting your weight on the back foot and leaning towards the wicket. You play forward to well-pitched-up bowling and back to short-pitched bowling.
rabbit	Poor or tail-end batsman.
run	A run is scored when the batsman hits the ball and runs the length of the pitch. If he fails to reach the popping crease before the ball is thrown in and the bails are taken off, he is 'run out'. Four runs are scored when the ball is hit across the boundary. Six runs are scored when it crosses the boundary without bouncing. This is how the umpire signals 'four' and 'six'.

four

six

If the batsman does not put his bat down inside the popping crease at the end of a run before setting off on another run, the umpire will signal 'one short' like this.

A run is then deducted from the total by the scorer.

stance

The stance is the way a batsman stands and holds his bat when he is waiting to receive a delivery. There are many different types of stance. For instance, 'side on', with the shoulder pointing down the wicket; 'square on', with the body turned towards the bowler; 'bat raised' and so on.

striker

The batsman who is receiving the bowling. The batsman at the other end is called the non-striker.

stumped

If you play and miss and the wicket-keeper knocks a bail off with the ball in his hands, you will be out 'stumped' if you are out of your crease.

ton

A century. One hundred runs scored by a batsman.

beamer   See **full toss**.

bouncer   The bowler pitches the ball very short and bowls it hard into the ground to get extra bounce and surprise the batsman. The ball will often reach the batsman at shoulder height or above. But you have to be a fast bowler to bowl a good bouncer. A slow bouncer is often called a 'long hop' and is easy to pull or cut for four.

full toss   A ball bowled which doesn't bounce before reaching the batsman is a full toss. Normally it's easy to score off a full toss, so it's considered a bad ball. A high full toss from a fast bowler is called a 'beamer'. It is very dangerous and should never be bowled deliberately.

googly   A 'googly' is an off-break bowled with a leg break action (see **leg break**) out of the back of the hand like this.

hat trick   Three wickets from three consecutive balls by one bowler. They don't have to be in the same over i.e. two wickets from the last two balls of one over and one from the first of the next.

half-volley   See **length**

leg break/   The 'leg break' is a delivery from a spinner
off-break   which turns from leg to off. An 'off-break'
                 turns from off to leg.

That's easy to remember when it's a right-hand bowler bowling to a right-hand batsman. But when a right-arm, off-break bowler bowls to a left-handed bat he is bowling leg-breaks. And a left-hander bowling with an off-break action bowls leg-breaks to a right-hander. It takes some working out – but the drawing helps.

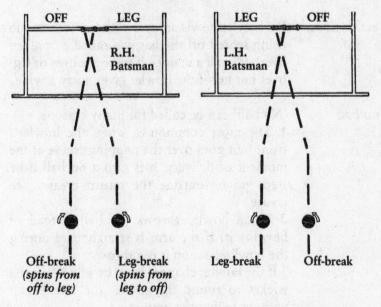

| OFF | LEG | LEG | OFF |

R.H. Batsman   L.H. Batsman

Off-break   Leg-break   Leg-break   Off-break
(spins from   *(spins from*
off to leg)   *leg to off)*

leg-cutter/   A ball which cuts away off the pitch from leg
off-cutter   to off-leg is a 'leg-cutter'. The 'off-cutter' goes
                 from off to leg. Both these deliveries are
                 bowled by fast or medium-pace bowlers. See
                 seam bowling.

leggie   Slang for a leg-spin bowler.

length   You talk about the 'length' or 'pitch' of a ball
                  bowled. A good length ball is one that makes
                  the batsman unsure whether to play back or
                  forward. A short-of-a-length ball pitches
                  slightly closer to the bowler than a good
                  length. A very short-pitched ball is called a
                  'long hop'. A 'half-volley' is an over-pitched
                  ball which bounces just in front of the bats-
                  man and is easy to drive.

long hop   A ball which pitches very short. See **length**.

maiden over   If a bowler bowls an over without a single run
                  being scored off the bat, it's called a 'maiden
                  over'. It's still a maiden if there are byes or leg-
                  byes but not if the bowler gives away a wide.

no ball   'No ball' can be called for many reasons.
                  1 The most common is when the bowler's
                  front foot goes over the popping crease at the
                  moment of delivery. It is also a no ball if he
                  steps on or outside the return crease. See
                  crease.
                  2 If the bowler throws the ball instead of
                  bowling it. If the arm is straightened during
                  the bowling action it is a throw.
                  3 If the bowler changes from bowling over the
                  wicket to round the wicket (or vice versa)
                  without telling the umpire.
                  4 If there are more than two fielders behind
                  square on the leg side. (There are other field-
                  ing regulations with the limited overs game.
                  For instance, the number of players who have
                  to be within the circle.)

A batsman can't be out off a no ball, except run out. A penalty of one run (an experiment of two runs is being tried in county cricket) is added to the score and an extra ball must be bowled in the over. The umpire shouts 'no ball' and signals like this:

over the wicket

If a right-arm bowler delivers the ball from the right of the stumps i.e. with his bowling arm closest to the stumps, then he is bowling 'over the wicket'. If he bowls from the other side of the stumps he is bowling 'round the wicket'.

pace

The pace of the ball is the speed it is bowled at. A fast or pace bowler like Waqar Younis can bowl at speeds of up to 90 miles an hour. The different speeds of bowlers range from fast through medium to slow with in-between speeds like fast-medium and medium-fast (fast-medium is the faster).

pitch

See **length**.

round the wicket

See **over the wicket**

seam The seam is the sewn, raised ridge which runs round a cricket ball.

seam bowling Bowling – usually medium to fast – where the ball cuts into or away from the batsman off the seam.

spell A 'spell' of bowling is the number of overs bowled in succession by a bowler. So if a bowler bowls six overs before being replaced by another bowler, he has bowled a spell of six overs.

swing bowling A cricket ball can be bowled to swing through the air. It has to be bowled in a particular way to achieve this and one side of the ball must be polished and shiny. Which is why you always see fast bowlers shining the ball. An 'in-swinger' swings into the batsman's legs from the off-side. An 'out-swinger' swings away towards the slips.

trundler A steady, medium-pace bowler who is not particularly good.

turn Another word for spin. You can say 'the ball turned a long way' or 'it spun a long way'.

wicket maiden An over when no run is scored off the bat and the bowler takes one wicket or more.

wide If the ball is bowled too far down the leg side or the off-side for the batsman to reach (usually the edge of the return crease is the line umpires look for) it is called a 'wide'. One run is added to the score and an extra ball is bowled in the over.

In limited overs cricket wides are given for balls closer to the stumps – any ball bowled down the leg side risks being called a wide in this sort of 'one-day' cricket.

This is how an umpire signals a wide.

yorker   A ball usually a fast one – bowled to bounce precisely under the batsman's bat. The most dangerous yorker is fired in fast towards the batsman's legs to hit leg stump.

FIELDING

backing up   A fielder backs up a throw to the wicket-keeper or bowler by making sure it doesn't go for overthrows. So when a throw comes in to the keeper, a fielder is positioned behind him to cover him if he misses it. Not to be confused with a *batsman* backing up.

chance   A catchable ball. So to miss a chance is the same as to drop a catch.

close/deep   Fielders are either placed close to the wicket (near the batsman) or in the deep or 'out-field' (near the boundary).

hole-out	A slang expression for a batsman being caught. 'He holed out at mid-on.'
overthrow	If the ball is thrown to the keeper or the bowler's end and is misfielded allowing the batsmen to take extra runs, these are called 'overthrows'.
silly	A fielding position very close to the batsman and in front of the wicket e.g. silly mid-on.
sledging	Using abusive language and swearing at a batsman to put him off. A slang expression – first used in Australia.
square	Fielders 'square' of the wicket are on a line with the batsman on either side of the wicket. If they are fielding further back from this line, they are 'behind square' or 'backward of square'; if they are fielding in front of the line i.e. closer to the bowler, they are 'in front of square' or 'forward of square'.
standing up/ standing back	The wicket-keeper 'stands up' to the stumps for slow bowlers. This means he takes his position immediately behind the stumps. For fast bowlers he stands well back – often several yards away for very quick bowlers. He may either stand up or back for medium-pace bowlers.

GENERAL WORDS

colts	County Colts teams are selected from the best young cricketers in the county at all ages from

Under 11 to Under 17. Junior league cricket is usually run by the County Colts Association.

under 11s/ 12s etc. You qualify for an Under 11 team if you are 11 or under on September 1st prior to the cricket season. So if you're 12 but you were 11 on September 1st last year, you can play for the Under 11s.

———————— • ————————

FIELDING POSITIONS

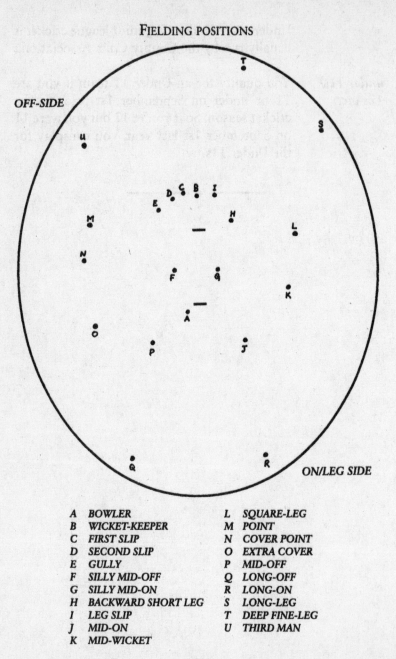

OFF-SIDE

ON/LEG SIDE

A	BOWLER	L	SQUARE-LEG
B	WICKET-KEEPER	M	POINT
C	FIRST SLIP	N	COVER POINT
D	SECOND SLIP	O	EXTRA COVER
E	GULLY	P	MID-OFF
F	SILLY MID-OFF	Q	LONG-OFF
G	SILLY MID-ON	R	LONG-ON
H	BACKWARD SHORT LEG	S	LONG-LEG
I	LEG SLIP	T	DEEP FINE-LEG
J	MID-ON	U	THIRD MAN
K	MID-WICKET		

GLORY
GARDENS
CRICKET CLUB

GLORY IN
THE CUP

BOB CATTELL

Hooker, Azzie, Erica and the rest all play cricket in their spare time, but they've never taken it very seriously until now. Kiddo, one of their school teachers, suggests they form an official team and play proper matches – and Glory Gardens C.C. is formed. Hooker, as captain, soon finds out that cricket teams weren't built in a day: some players squabble, some can't catch, and some have tantrums and go home at half-time! So will Glory Gardens go all out for victory . . . or will they be out for a duck?

ISBN – 978 0 099 46111 1
RED FOX
£4.99

GLORY
GARDENS
CRICKET CLUB

THE BIG
TEST

BOB CATTELL

It really doesn't look like being Hooker's season.
Not only does he spend the first match of the league
suffering a dropped-catch jinx but now there's civil
war in the team over the selections. Sometimes
captaining the Glory Gardens Cricket Team isn't
the fun you might think. It's not the matches that
prove the most trouble for poor Hooker – it's the
infighting. He has one solution that might work.
But making Ohbert captain in his place?
That's not strategy – that's suicide.

ISBN – 978 0 099 22342 9
RED FOX
£4.99

GLORY
GARDENS
CRICKET CLUB

WORLD CUP
FEVER

BOB CATTELL

Glory Gardens C.C. can't resist a challenge and this
time they're going for gold in a World Cup competition!
With teams from Barbados and South Africa visiting the
area at the same time, it's a brilliant opportunity for the
club to make its mark worldwide. It's not long before the
thrills and spills of cricket spark off sporting drama,
temper tantrums and practical jokes. So, as Australia
do battle with the West Indies and South Africa face
India, can Glory Gardens rise above the squabbling
and bring glory for England . . . ?

ISBN – 978 0 099 17842 2
RED FOX
£4.99

GLORY
GARDENS
CRICKET CLUB

LEAGUE OF
CHAMPIONS

BOB CATTELL

GLORY GARDENS C.C. are back and this time the stakes are high as they play to win in the League of Champions! Hooker and co have got to get their act together fast if they're going to make it through the early rounds to the final of the knock-out competition. And let's face it, with Ohbert on the team it's not as straightforward as it might seem. As the competition progresses, the pressure builds and the team realise they are going to have to pull out all the stops if they want to make it all the way to the top . . . and Edgbaston!

ISBN – 978 0 099 72401 8
RED FOX
£4.99

GLORY GARDENS CRICKET CLUB

BLAZE OF GLORY

BOB CATTELL

GLORY GARDENS C.C. are Barbados bound for the cricket tour of a lifetime. Having begged, scrimped and saved for months they've finally got the cash together to take the team to the sunny Caribbean. Playing the top teams from the island, they find cricketing West Indian style rather tricky. What with rock-hard pitches and startlingly fast bowlers, if they don't seriously improve their form, it looks as if the Glory Gardens' players may have finally met their match . . .

ISBN – 978 0 099 72411 7
RED FOX
£4.99

GLORY GARDENS CRICKET CLUB

DOWN THE WICKET

BOB CATTELL

On returning from their West Indies tour, the players in
GLORY GARDENS C.C. are devastated to learn that
their ground has been sold. Although the senior club
disbands, the team are determined to find a new home
and, led by Jo, they vote to play the season's league
games on the recreation ground where the club
first began. But the pitch is dreadful, the changing
rooms a disgrace and, with their best batsmen
threatening to leave, some drastic action
is called for . . .

ISBN – 978 0 099 40903 8

RED FOX

£4.99

GLORY
GARDENS
CRICKET CLUB

THE GLORY
ASHES

BOB CATTELL

When Ohbert creates a GLORY GARDENS website,
unknown to everyone else, his mission is to make them
the most famous junior club in the world! His claims for
the club get bigger and bigger until one day he puts out a
challenge for anyone to come and beat the 'reigning world
champions' – and the top young club in Australia approach
them to do just that. A tournament is arranged, but when
the press pick up on the story, there is much more at
stake than just their reputation . . .

ISBN – 978 0 099 40904 5
RED FOX
£4.99